Trut

1

Truth and Grace

By: Jennifer Goodin

ISBN-13: 978-1496111265

Acknowledgements:

There are many people to thank in the production of this novel. First, my family, Keith and Elisabeth for putting up with the hours and stress put into this work. You make me want to make you as proud of me as I am of you. Also, to my angel son, Christopher, thank you for showing me how to act in dignity and humor even during the worst of times. It was your example of living life to the very fullest that inspired me to finally write down the story that has been in my head. Thank you to Danielle Garriot and The Anchor Project for helping me learn the publishing process. Also thank you to: Tina Spencer, Bonnie Cuddie, Lisa Graham, Andy Jennings, Matthew Ryan Lail and Sue Jackson for the first draft read and response. Finally, thank you to Lori Eaton for the final draft edit. Without each of you, this book would not be complete.

Characters (in alphabetical order)

Callaway (Daddy): Lavani's father, Sarah's husband, twin to Colton

Charlotte (Chandrika): Sarah's mother

Christian: Lavani and Steve's deceased son

Colton: Callaway's twin brother

Emily: Lavani and Steve's 21 year old daughter

Father (Mr. Teague): Sarah's father; Honey's 1st husband

Father (Thompson): Callaway and Colton's father

Honey: Sarah's "stepmother" and best friend

Jay: Lavani's brother; twin to Jayce

Jayce: Lavani's sister; twin to Jay

Kevin: Lavani's first love; friend

Lavani: main character; mother, wife, care-taker

Leonard: Honey's 2nd husband

Martha: Sarah's sister

Molly: Sarah's best friend in high school

Natalie: Nurse-midwife; Sarah's friend

Patti: Lavani's high school friend

Ruth: Sarah's sister

Sarah (Momma): Lavani's mother, mid-wife, cancer patient

Steve: Lavani's husband

Dedicated to: Elisabeth, my angel on earth, and Christopher, my angel in Heaven.

Truth and Grace

Part One:

Lavani's Story

CHAPTER ONE:

I never knew for sure if my mother loved me.

She clothed me, fed me, took good care of me, and oversaw my education; but, a certain lack of ease in her when near me betrayed her mixed feelings. I didn't observe this same dichotomy in her relationship with my brother and sister. I would turn quickly at times, to find her staring intently at me, as if trying to figure out who, or rather, what I was. There remained the slightest of hesitations before she hugged me or touched me. But, when she did, the hug felt warm and long with a gently caressing touch.

Our relationship of mixed signals lasted almost my entire life. Honestly, no one called me an "easy" child. I felt awkward in my own skin, like it never fit correctly, and plain-faced surrounded by beauties. I possessed a terrible habit of asking all the wrong questions at all the wrong times. Momma tended to jump to negative conclusions and said things that hurt my feelings. Her patience level with me seemed less than with everyone else. I desperately wanted to be like my beautiful Momma, fairy like in build and beautiful even in her elder years, with her long, dark hair and chocolate brown eyes. So, an element of jealousy from my side, combined with her hesitation, became fodder for a contentious relationship. Maybe that explained my surprise when she asked me to come stay with her.

I am Lavani Rose Thompson -Trimble, or, more popularly, Vani. I am forty-four and three quarters years old. Most people quit counting their years in quarters after they reach sixteen, but I would break it down to the hours before turning forty-five. To me, that age represented the beginning of the end, the start of being elderly, the tip off of the hill and rolling on down, so I fought it. I am, first of all a mother of two, well I should say one, no I am the mother of two children, one living and one, well, not. I am a wife, sister, daughter, cousin and friend. Except for a three year break, I've taught English since the age of twenty-two at both the high school and community college level. Until this past summer, I've always thought those words defined me. I've seen tragedy in my life and experienced joy, like everyone and simply quit expecting anything more out of life until I received a phone call from my mother that changed my life.

As usual, I stood at my stove in the kitchen, this time making strawberry jelly when my phone rang. I wiped my hands on my apron then answered, scowling at the smear of hot jelly I left on the screen of my new iphone.

"Lavani?" my momma always called me by my full name, she never called anyone by a nickname. As her cool voice drifted out of the telephone, I already felt disheveled. I smoothed my hair down into my ratty ponytail and wiped my face with the towel tucked into my apron pocket. Since I was also using it as a rag while cooking, I ended up just getting sticky strawberry goo on my face. I imagined her sigh of disappointment if she saw me in my ratty tee shirt with the hole in the front and my cut off sweat pants, the zebra stripe apron with bleach spots all over, covering my entire ensemble.

"Yes. Hi Mom, how are you?"

"Well, I'm doing alright. You've just been on my mind today and I thought I'd give you a call to see what you were doing."

"I'm canning some strawberry jelly. Would you like me to bring you some when we come visit on Sunday?" The Sunday visit remains a southern tradition. All over the south, we go to church, then visit our mothers, provided they are within driving distance. Momma lived only thirty minutes away, so it was an obligation to go.

We'd arrive around 12:45 to a table filled with one of three meals: fried chicken, mashed potatoes, peas, corn and gravy; or roast beef, carrots and potatoes all cooked in a thick broth with gravy and broccoli; or Fried pork chops, green beans, scalloped potatoes, and fruit salad. We knew which meal it would be when we walked into the house simply by sniffing the air. Her foods always smelled and looked as good as they tasted. She used herbs from her garden and everything she served grew on the farm. The tradition comforted, in its own way. It would have been sacrilege to eat anywhere else, or anything else. Say Momma made a lasagna one Sunday instead, it would have been perfectly good, but something about the week would have been thrown off and everyday would be odd until we returned to her house for the "real meal" the following Sunday. Several times we insisted she not cook and would take her out to a restaurant we wanted her to try, but nothing ever tasted as good as her food.

"That would be nice. Ummmm ... I ... You.." my mother's uncharacteristic stumbling and hesitating concerned me.

"Momma, are you OK? What's going on?" I asked.

"Nothing, really. I just... I was ..."

"What?" I questioned, worried now.

"I was hoping maybe you could come stay awhile with me this summer. I have to have a little procedure done and the doctor said I needed to ask someone to stay with me a few days afterward and I know you are off all summer this year. And, with Emily being gone this summer, she won't be home to take care of. But, I know you don't want to spend it being a nurse, after..., well anyway, I shouldn't have asked, it's too much. Never mind, Lavani." * I could hear her becoming uncomfortable, her voice stiffened and became even more formal with each word she uttered.

"Mom, slow down. Of course I can come stay with you. What procedure are you having done? When? Why? You are leaving me with lots of questions, here." This was just like her, she always trivialized any kind of medical issues, like if she denied illness, it couldn't happen. In

15

fact, because of her and Daddy's stubbornness, we didn't even know he had heart issues until he never woke up one bitter cold morning.

"Well, the docs think I have a little bit of cancer, so the Doctor wants to remove it and then try some treatments to see if she can..."

"CANCER??? What kind of cancer?" I abruptly sat on a kitchen chair.

"Well, it's not all that bad, it's female cancer, you know." I could almost hear her blushing over the phone, strange because my mom served as a nurse-midwife for years, she taught us the proper terminology for all the female parts (and male) instead of any of the cute words my friends used. In middle school when my friends were using terms like 'dick' and 'pussy' as curse words, I didn't even know what parts of the body they were talking about!

"Momma, be more specific, please," I begged.

"It's possibly ovarian cancer. They think it could be in an advanced stage because of my age. I've agreed to the surgery. They will go in and look for cancer at first, if they find it they will do a radical hysterectomy, like you had, but I'm not sure about any treatments at this point. I just don't know if I want to do that at my age."

Silence fell between us, I knew this diagnosis at my mother's age loomed practically as a death sentence. From my own experience, I knew the difficulty of recovery from that type of surgery, and I wasn't sure she would be strong enough to heal afterward. Tears gathered at the back of my throat and thickened my voice, "When?"

"The surgery is Monday. I went to my doctor for a check-up and after telling her about some symptoms I was having, she scheduled me for a pelvic exam then an internal ultrasound. Both of those came back with abnormal findings, so Dr. Kelly set me up with a gynecological oncologist in Lexington. I saw her last week and we set everything up. Her name is Dr. Rose."

"Last week? Mom, why didn't you tell me? I could have been there for you." I live close to Lexington! She had been in town, seen the doctor and driven away without even letting me know.

"Well, Honey was with me, and she is willing to take care of me, I just think it is too much for her at her age. And besides"

"Besides?" I asserted.

"Well, besides, I just wanted you," she said with hope.

"Me? Really?" I couldn't help the incredulity in my voice and it must have conveyed through the telephone. I wanted to say, 'You can't stop to see me while you are in town, but it's OK if I come and take care of you? Are you ashamed of being seen with me or something? I mean, I know I'm not pretty like my brother and sister, but really?'

Of course, I didn't say anything of the sort,that would be disrespectful to my mother, a reason for yet, another lecture and she wouldn't let me help her. *Did I want to help her? I mean, we never really had what someone could call, a strong mother-daughter relationship.* The memories of arguments and disagreement and that smoldering resentment that arises between two people rose into my throat and chocked me a little. I heard her voice continuing on.

"It's OK if you already have plans, I understand. I can ask your sister, or the ladies from the church. I just thought maybe we could, you know, talk and stuff." Her voice was already stiff with the assumption, I would say no. Stiffness and stoicism were her defense mechanisms. I guess she inherited that from my grandmother (her mother) who was a full-blooded Cherokee.

'Talk and stuff?' Who was this lady, using such hip terminology? She was usually so proper, her lecture went something like "You already have enough going against you, being from Kentucky where everyone in the world thinks you are an uneducated Hillbilly. Don't add to your troubles by confirming that impression with improper grammar and non-specific language. Hmmm... my students have heard that lecture many many times 'Mirror, mirror on the wall, I am my mother after all.'

"Mom, I will be there. I will pack a bag and come up Sunday and plan to stay several weeks. After that, we will see." I didn't finish the statement with, '*and God help us, every one*,' but I sure wanted to!

I could hear the relief in her voice as she sighed, "Thank you."

We talked a few more minutes about the farm and people I knew back home, then hung up. I went back to my jelly, but my mind kept echoing the conversation. Cancer. I wanted you. Cancer. Talk and stuff. Cancer. My jelly didn't turn out as well as usual. Some people who ate it, said it tasted a little salty.

Truth and Grace

CHAPTER TWO:

That evening, when my husband, Steve, came home from work, his favorite dinner sat ready. I spread the drop leaf table in the kitchen with a simple white tablecloth. I set it with two place settings and put the food in bowls, for the first time in months, since Emily stayed, actually, I planned a good dinner and a little seduction. Funny how, even after twenty-five years of marriage, sex still greased the wheels, if I wanted something. I wore his favorite color, a blue shirt everyone said made me look thinner. I fixed my hair and put on some make up, just so I would look my best for him. Actually, I looked forward to the seduction. I would let him eat, of course, while some soft music played in the background, maybe something jazzy and full of saxophones. Then, he would stand up and offer me his hand and we would dance really close from the kitchen into the living room and then, into the bedroom shutting the door to the world. We would make long and slow love and he would tell me how much he loved me, how beautiful he still found me and he would focus upon my pleasure. OK, so he never danced, and didn't like jazz, and we had sex, never love, but it could happen, at least in my fantasy.

Steve, with wet hands and hair, walked into the kitchen straight from the little bathroom off of the garage next to the laundry room and grabbed an "every day" plate from the cabinet, loaded it down with fried chicken, mashed potatoes topped with gravy, and creamed peas straight from the early garden. He didn't even see the table all set so prettily, or me in my low cut shirt, with make up on and my hair fixed like he liked it. He just came in and I stood, stunned, as he took his plate into the living room and turned on the Indians game. He settled down into his battered leather chair, put a towel over the arm of it and began eating. "Well," I thought, "if you can't beat them, join them," so I brought in his glass of sweet tea and asked, "Steve, Honey, can we talk for a minute?"

"In a little bit, Vani, I'm tired and I want to see this game, the Indians are challenging for first place."

"Steve, my mom called today..."

"Vani," it will wait, this game won't," he turned away from me and put his plate on the arm of the chair. "Hey, get me a fork, I forgot mine."

I went and got his fork, brought it to him then took my plate and ate it at the kitchen table, alone. As always, while I ate I played out the fantasies in my head. In my mind, I lived with a pseudo husband. He looked like a grown up version of my high school boyfriend, Kevin. Through the years, he aged as I did, and his interests and hobbies changed as I wanted them to. This pseudo husband of mine appeared perfect to me: romantic, handy, fun, everything I wanted. I visualized him sitting across the table from me, staring deep into my eyes with his bright blues as he slowly enjoyed each bite he ate. We talked of everything, his exotic job, my amazing cooking ability, current events, politics, even religion and we never argued. He would lean over and kiss me randomly, patting my hand with the passion of his words, and then he would suddenly interrupt himself to exclaim how beautiful I looked tonight. He got up to help me with the dishes and the kitchen chores, until with the kitchen clean, he drew me into his arms and we danced to the low music, kissing and holding each other. We blew out the candles and, he disappeared. I came out of my fantasy with a sigh and a smile for my own foolishness. I mean, seriously, how many women my age still possessed imaginary friends? I thought about my first love, a young boy, a couple of years older than me. We attended the same high school. When I first saw him, I fell in love. He was so cute, with dark hair and blue eyes. He possessed a zest for life that drew me to him. He drove the fastest car in town, worked and lived on a farm, played baseball and loved me. We went everywhere together during those days. We even worked in the fields together, just to see each other during the busy times on a farm. He loved to be romantic, flowers for no reason, sweet words whispered in my ears, dancing outside when no music played. I loved him beyond distraction. I thought all men were like him, and all women were as eager as I was to experience it all. I gave him my virginity in the back seat of his Mustang and he took it with reverence and care. I never regretted it.

I'm around people all day long, high school kids, other teachers (younger teachers) but inside I'm alone, living in my perfect little fantasy world. My friends have so much to do with their own families, I haven't felt comfortable calling them to do things with me. Honestly, I didn't want to do anything anyway. I stayed home and canned food I gave away, gardened vegetables that the neighbors ate more of than we did. I read and dreamed about all the ways I was going to remodel my house. I kept it clean, like I never had before and the laundry done and the beds made, but there was no joy in it. I did it to have something to do.

This summer had been especially brutal for me. Thinking Emily would be home for those three precious months, I decided not to teach. Besides, the summer English classes became loaded with those great big boys, with foul mouths and terrible attitudes. I just didn't feel like dealing with their excuses. The girls, just as bad, or worse, dramatized everything. I'm so sick of high school drama. Every year it's, "Mrs. Trimble, she's talking bad about me, I need to go to the counselor." Or they cried over, fought for, and competed to catch the big bad boy's attention. This summer, I wanted to do something different. I made vague plans of spending time on the beach, of shopping more, painting my living room. I don't know, maybe dynamiting it would be better.

I walked through the house collecting dishes and picking up for the night. I put Steve's fork, plate and glass into the dishwasher with mine and the pots and pans from cooking, it still wasn't a full load, so I decided to wait until after breakfast in the morning to run it. I knew he would have a snack before bed, and that would help fill up the load. I picked up the newspaper and put it into the recycling bin, then put Steve's shoes in the closet. I started a load of laundry, and then nothing needed doing. So, I went to the other side of the house. I stood in Emily's door for a long time, just looking in. Her bedroom, typical Emily, shone in a bright pink and lime green with a zebra bedspread thrown haphazardly over the bed. The window shades, pulled up high, let in lots of sunshine and highlighted dust motes in the air. They looked like little diamonds in the late evening sun. Trophies, crowns, medals and assorted make up brushes covered her dresser and shelves. Her closet held only winter clothes. She came home from college over spring break to regale us with tales of her college days. Dances, homework, study groups, the archery team, her new boyfriend, and her roommates filled the conversations we had. She talked long and fast, filling us with her brand of sunshine and joy, slept late, ate like a teen aged boy, changed out her wardrobe and left with her little VW convertible packed to the rag top with everything she needed for school's final weeks.

I still saw her in there, though. I visualized her around the age of ten playing with her Barbie Dream house she received from Santa Clause that year. It stood about three feet high, full of the fragile plastic pieces of furniture considered to be cool. She dressed her Barbie in a long white wedding dress with red high heel shoes and put her in the driver's side of the Barbie convertible her brother gave her. "Come on, Ken, we're late for our wedding," she said in a false voice, I guess she thought sounded more mature. Ken bounced out of the house (in Emily's hand). In a bass voice she announced, "Wait for me, Gorgeous! You need me for the wedding!" He slid into the car wearing a pair of dark jeans and a brown coat with no shirt. Well, usually we called him Naked Ken, so this was an upgrade. She drove the car around until she noticed me standing in the doorway, she grinned that lightning grin and said, "Mom, want to come play with me?" Sometimes I did, and I played Skipper and Kelly, the bridesmaid and the ring bearer, and sometimes I refused. I wish I chose to play more when given the chance.

Through the years, her room changed, the Barbie Doll House went to the attic and a beginner sewing machine took its place. Then boy band posters lined the walls, as she giggled on the phone with a girlfriend over all the cute guys at school with fashion magazines lined on the floor as they planned shopping trips. She grew up so fast. I know it's a cliché but time runs so quickly. I turned around to find an empty house in college, with she and her brother both gone on their different journeys. The echo of her laughter, her tears, her giggles, her play hung in the room as tangible to me as the zebra comforter and graduation photos slipped into the mirror on the top of the dresser.

The day before she left, I was drinking coffee on the front porch watching my neighbor roto till his garden and thinking, how lucky that my spring break had fallen at the same time as hers. I looked up to see her standing beside me, uncharacteristically quiet with her hands wrapped around a steaming cup of coffee, "Mom, can we talk?"

"Sure," I scooted over and she sat beside me on the old porch swing. I smiled as I noticed that she pushed us along faster and faster as she gathered the courage to say whatever she needed to say to me. It was so Emily, all motion and movement.

"Mom, I've been offered a really cool opportunity for the summer. My advisor really thinks I should take it, but I don't know if I should or not, or what you might think of it." She continued in a rush of words, "They think I'm really good with my fashion design and I have been offered a chance to internship with a company in New York for the summer. They think it would look really good on my resume if I did it and, well, I really want to. Addy's folks live near New York and have a guest house that they have offered to let us live in free of rent. She knows her way around the city and really wants to go home for the summer. I think it would be an amazing opportunity and help my career someday. I just wanted to check with you. I know summers are bad for you, and I want to be here for you, but I really want to do this too."

I looked, really looked at this daughter of mine, with the deep green eyes pleading with me to understand and give her my blessing. How lucky I am, I thought, to have such a child – a woman now – who would seek my thoughts still even at the age of twenty-one. I saw her sitting there in the swing with her long sunny hair caught in a messy ponytail at the nape of her neck, with her beautiful face naked of any cosmetics, and her hands tightly clasped around her coffee cup as she nervously awaited my answer

"Of course you must go! This is an incredible opportunity for you and something you've been waiting for all your life! GO! But, you know I'm going to come visit and go to a Broadway show and make sure you are behaving, right?"

She laughed and hugged me tight, dropping a little of her hot coffee down my arm as she sighed in relief, "Thanks, Mom, I knew you'd understand, you always have." And she jumped up, "I have to call Addy!" She ran into the house and I stayed on the front porch for a long time, looking at the newly turned earth in my neighbor's garden, a brown scar on the perfect green of his lawn that would, in time, be filled with beautiful plants. I thought of how Child-Emily would run into his garden and thump his watermelons and exclaim, "This one is ripe, I'm sure of it!" And, every year, he would bring her the first ripe watermelon, even though we had a row of them in our own back yard. Who would he bring his melon to this year? I wondered. Then, I went into the house to refill my coffee cup and start the day's chores.

Sorting laundry later that day, it struck me, at Emily's age, I had been a bride. Halfway through college I married Steve because I discovered Christian was on the way. Even six weeks pregnant, I didn't tell anyone for fear of their disappointment. I think my momma still believed I should have worn that white dress in the church. I prayed to not vomit on the preacher during the vows and to escape from the lightning that should have struck! I spent the entire honeymoon throwing up and having sex because Steve didn't think pregnancy was any excuse for not enjoying his honeymoon.

Before I walked down that aisle, I wanted to scream, "NO!" but, I didn't know how to do it; I couldn't imagine seeing myself raising a child alone, or disappointing my parents. I determined to change Steve, I convinced myself his love for me would make him a gentleman and a companion. He was the second man I ever made love with, and the excitement of sneaking around playing a major part of our relationship. I never even thought about the fact that we never really went on a date together, or even had much conversation unless it circled around him and his activities. Not much changed in life. I sure didn't change him, and we still talked mostly about him.

With a crack of a bat and the roar of a crowd from the television, I came back to myself. The Indians were winning 3-1 in the 5th inning and my husband soundly slept leaning back in his recliner. I shut Emily's door. Then I stood next to the closed door across from hers. If I could bring myself to open it, I would find a clean room, a KY Wildcats bedspread neatly covering the double bookcase bed, his trophies and medals sitting on top of the shelf we built at the top of the room. I would see his books, neatly arranged in a bookcase and an unfinished model car sitting on his desk, gathering dust and waiting for that last coat of varnish and the glue to put the tiny seats and gearshift in. Feeling tears already gathering in my eyes, I patted the door instead and whispered, "I love you," then quickly walked into the living room. I picked up my book and went into my bedroom to read and write in my journal.

I learned this habit from my mother. She wrote almost every night in scores of lined black composition books. She never let us read them, but sometimes we saw the pictures she drew on the pages. I didn't draw in mine, I didn't get her talent, and I used pretty journals that caught my eye. In fact, I probably stored so many in the

35

basement, I never needed to buy another. I always found my pretty journals a release. I encouraged my students to do so as well. Emily also kept a journal, Christian had off and on. I entered in the events of the day and my thoughts, then opened my book to where I left off earlier in the day.

I didn't hear Steve's recliner hit the ground. Usually, I heard it from the bedroom shut the book and turned out the light in time to fake sleep. This time, I looked up as the door opened. "Why are you still awake?" he asked.

"I got caught up in my book. It's a really good one." I responded. I prayed he wasn't going to want sex. My stomach twisted, I hated when he wanted sex after ignoring me the rest of the day. He never understood that foreplay, for me, began with conversation and attention. For him, foreplay began when he touched my body. I nonchalantly turned off the lamp and settled on my left side, facing away from him, when he slid into bed. "Please don't touch me, please don't touch me, please don't touch me," dammit he rolled over and put his hand on my hip. "I'm really not in the mood, Steve," I said.

"You are never in the mood."

"I just don't feel good," I lied.

"You feel good to me," his hand slid up to my breast and pinched my nipple.

"Steve, I really don't want sex," I insisted.

"Well, I do," he responded and pulled my shirt up over my head. Unfortunately, this situation happened a great deal in our married lives. Arguing resulted in him verbally pushing me and getting rougher and rougher touching me. The times I continued to refuse, he stopped, but remained furious for days. He yelled at me for everything, pouted and called me frigid or a terrible wife. He insulted me about everything, I was a bad housekeeper, cook, mother, wife, whatever he thought of, until the next time he wanted sex and I gave in. I chose to give in most times, lie there and let him have his way. It wasn't worth it, I rolled over on my back and he had sex. We didn't have sex, he did. He touched me where he liked to touch, then pushed inside me, grunting at my dryness. He talked dirty to me, using words and phrases I hated, like he thought that would help, and eventually reached climax. I realized as he rolled off, he never kissed me. Not on the lips, the face, the neck, nothing. Just a rough hand and sex.

I hated myself afterwards, "Why was I so weak? Where was my strength to just get up and go to the other room? What did it matter if he was angry? This was still my body and it should be my decision." The thing of it was, I wanted to make love earlier. I wanted his touch, I wanted his attention. I think he withheld it because he sensed I did want it, and this helped him control his world.

Steve liked to accuse me of using sex as a weapon. I admit, I did use it to get things I wanted from him, especially when I was younger. But now, I simply didn't want him. I used to read all the magazine articles about how to keep a man happy and improve our sex life.

After some difficult sessions, I made a nice dinner, on a day with no sport scheduled and started a conversation about sex. It ended up being short and testy, rather than the promised hot and sexy.

"Steve, I need to talk about sex with you," I started.

"Oh yes, one of my favorite topics," he winked.

"I think you are a great lover," the magazine insisted I should start this way, "and I don't want to change much, but there are a couple of things you do that I would like to try a different way," I started shaking, his eyes had gone cold. I told him the two things I didn't like, and asked him to try to different things I thought I would like.

He finished his dinner and put his napkin on the table, pulled me to my feet, and I swear to you, did both of the things I asked him not too. I protested, "But, Steve,,,"

"Shut up, I know what I'm doing," he insisted. I researched this, which meant he saw it on a porn site on the internet. "Women like this."

"I don't,"

"You will if you gave it a try instead of talking and getting all stiff."

I realized the fruitlessness of the conversation. We had sex and he did everything the same way as before Right before going to sleep he asked, "How many times did you orgasm?"

"Mmmmm," was the only thing I could come up with.

"That's what I thought," he said in a sleepy voice, "see, I told you I knew what I was doing. Get me some water when you get up to turn off the light."

I burned that magazine.

Truth and Grace

CHAPTER THREE:

I like to drive topless. Feeling the air rush over my body and through my hair relieves stress for me. It just makes me happy. My friends and colleagues call my little convertible my "mid-life" crisis car, but I don't care, I like it. It makes me feel good. On Sunday, I skipped church, packed my car with my suitcase, purse and make up bag, put the top down and took off for home. Home. Why is it that where we reside as adults is never quite the same? I lived in that same house on Milford Court, for almost 20 years, yet, it never felt as homey as the one I headed to now.

The tiny three bedroom, one bath house sitting on almost 200 acres of farmland with a pond full of crappie and bluegill and the woods adjacent to the pastures, would always ring with the peace of home. I drove down the interstate, hair flying wildly in the wind, slightly above the speed limit thinking of going home and feeling like a kid, forgetting for the moment I was an overweight, under-tall, middle aged woman with gray in her hair, a deep crease in her forehead, and crinkles beside her eyes. I turned up the radio and tapped along to the beat on the side of my car, enjoying every single mile I travelled.

I told Steve the day before (during a rain out delay, before the violent 80's movie started) about my mother's request. I expected his response, "Well, that's fine. How long will you be gone? A couple of weeks? That's crazy, she won't want you that long. What am I supposed to eat? Who's going to keep the laundry and house? I have to work, you know." This was always his excuse to not do stuff around the house. He *worked*. He constantly said, "Teachers don't really work for a living. You just babysit mostly. You have easy hours and no physical labor involved. I don't know why you always bitch about it, you go and play." Once, after I "played" many hours at school then came home to care for the baby and the house I lost my temper. He spent his days off golfing and playing softball, so I went on strike. I let everything in our tiny apartment go. I didn't do the dishes, let the laundry pile up, quit cooking and didn't pick up after either of us. The apartment smelled gross and looked filthy. He just ignored it and ignored me when I informed him of my strike until he started to help. Then, his mother called one day and said she and his father were coming to visit. He smirked at me, "Guess you will have to clean now, huh?" as he sat in his recliner.

"Nope, they are not my parents," I replied while continuing to grade 9th grade essays.

We sat there for a few minutes until he jumped up, cursing, from his chair. He stalked into the kitchen, filled the sink with hot water and a long stream of dish soap, grabbed a glass, stuck it into the water, then jammed his hand and washcloth into it. The glass burst, cutting his hand in a long jagged gash. I drove him to the emergency room and listened to the nurses coo and fuss over him, "You are so lucky to have a man who would do dishes," they said as the doctor stitched his hand.

The final blow came when the doc said, "Now, no housecleaning at least until the stitches come out!" as he winked at my husband in that man to man code they have.

After we got home, I cleaned the apartment while he made comments from the couch as he watched a basketball game on the tube. It became his favorite joke to tell on me. I laugh along, but inside it still pisses me off.

With that memory in mind, I assured him I knew he had to work, I already paid the teen aged boy across the road to mow the yard, twice a week for four weeks and the housekeeper the lady next door used to come in every three days to do laundry and dishes and pick up the house and there were meals frozen and labeled in the freezer. He grumbled about having people in the house and then his movie started, so he turned to it and I went into the bedroom to pack. I considered packing up and just leaving, wouldn't it be great to have my own little place? Truly, taking care of him seemed like taking care of another child, one that demanded and insisted but didn't return. I wanted him to be a companion and a friend. But, we possessed nothing in common. Even politically we stood on opposite sides. I voted Democrat, he voted Republican. I tended towards liberal, he leaned conservative. I enjoyed books, he enjoyed movies. I liked plays, he liked ballgames. I preferred to walk for exercise, he preferred to play basketball and golf and softball and flag football and lift weights. No wonder I resorted to my "Pseudo Husband." I held long conversations with him about the books I read and the politicians I detested. He walked beside me as I went around the neighborhood, I dreamed of the plays and symphonies we "attended" in my mind. This pseudo husband listened to me, to my desires and thoughts and ideas and supported them and encouraged me to do better, reach higher, try more. Yet, he accepted me where I landed and how I looked.

Is it too much to ask to have a relationship like that? I shook my head and continued with the chores I set for myself before going to take care of my mother. I called Emily to tell her about the situation and we discussed that she needed to stay in New York, if it became too bad, she could always fly in.

I finished packing then made sure I had everything checked off my list: clothes packed, check. Dishes washed and put away, check. Laundry finished, check. Then Steve came into the room and closed the door. Sex, check. My "To-do" list was checked off and everything was ready for me to go.

When did sex become something on the to-do list? I wondered again, what happened to the passion, the interest in our relationship? My husband literally bored me. When he started telling one of his "back in the good ole days" stories, I felt my eyes glaze over, I swear I silently recited the stories along with him. Except, every time he told one, his part grew just a little bit better, he got a little bit stronger, a little bit faster. I snickered, remembering him telling a story to his buddy, Brent, the other night, "You know I played quarterback in college. My team was undefeated all four years." He went on and on about who played what position and how big they all were and how they just insisted, he be the quarterback because it was his throwing arm that made them win. He forgot to mention that the "football" league he starred in was the flag football inter-mural league. I used to tease him that he could make a short story, long. It seemed that each of his stories just kept getting longer and longer. He added every detail to make himself a hero, and whoever he talked to would, eventually, look around frantically as they planned what to say to escape the room. When he finished, he would launch into another long story about being at work and how they couldn't function without him there to keep everyone in line. Then another story, then another. It seemed he had to impress any man with his importance at work. I called them his "wag the wiener" stories. Eventually, none of our couple friends came over to play cards or went out to eat with us anymore. One friend finally confessed, "Honestly, Vani, Ken (her husband) just really doesn't like Steve all that much. If it's OK with you, maybe just you and I could do things together." We tried to keep up with each other, but faded away too as responsibilities and life pulled us apart. In fact, other than family on holidays, and Emily's friends, no one visited us anymore. Was it all Steve? I wondered. Probably not. For a long time I couldn't talk to anyone about anything other than the shallowest of topics, or I would end up crying or, worse, in a full blown panic attack. I even, for the first year after losing Christian, cried every time the phone rang. Talk about a great way to scare off the salesmen, though!

I never believed in divorce, it just didn't factor into my worldview, but lately, I have been fantasizing what it would be like to be a widow. I really don't want him to die, I swear I don't. I do love him; but, well, it sure would be nice to move out of the big house he insisted we needed and move into a small condo and do things I wanted to do without someone being disagreeable about everything. I could go on those trips with the travel club at school over the summer without him shutting me down every time I mentioned it with, "We're broke! We can't afford that!" I couldn't buy a new pair of shoes without him yelling at me, for days. I couldn't leave the dinner dishes without listening to him rant on about how he had to work and do everything around the house when he put his plate into the dishwasher. And, he does have great life insurance. You know, I'm starting to wonder why I don't believe in divorce. Maybe, considering his family's medical history, I could just start serving more fried pork chops and chicken legs...

Shaking my head at my terrible thoughts, I merged onto the familiar exit, leading towards the home-place. Soon after, I turned into the long drive leading toward the house where I grew up. The day had turned slightly cloudy and a grey mist hung over the mountains behind the house and barns of home. I stopped the car and wished for the talent to paint the picture that lay before me. The house stood in the middle with plain white wood siding that needed paint. A wide red door opened to the breeze with two windows, also open, on each side, cooled the house. I loved the deep front porch with the light green swing gently moving in the rising air of the storm. Two rocking chairs and a small table waited for us to sit there with our glasses of iced tea. The cushions on the rocking chairs and the porch swing bloomed with a bright floral pattern, heavily leaning to reds and oranges and the plants and flowers my Momma loved surrounded the three sides of the porch that jutted out from the house. The white Rose of Sharon blossomed right next to the porch, with the green of the Hosta plants interspersed to provide a dense backdrop; in front of those happy red geraniums waved with silver mounds between each and in front of those petunias nodded and danced over the heads of the spreading phlox. A picture of color and texture graced the front of the plain appearance of the home and made it beautiful. Behind the house, two barns and a shed of an indeterminate gray color proudly housed the crops and behind those, where I could only see with my memory's eye, lay the orchards and the bee houses. Between the barns, the kitchen and herb gardens spread. Beyond all of that stood the kudzu covered wall of the mountain.

This was home, where I ran wild as a child, exploring the woods and up the mountain to the small mine where my dad, and later my brother, picked out the coal we needed for the winter heat. My parents expected me to help pick apples and peaches from the trees, and tomatoes and the green beans from the vine and dig potatoes and the carrots from the earth. I fed the cows, pigs, chicken and turkeys, but I never could bear to be around, when they butchered. I also helped can, freeze, smoke or store our efforts, so that we survived the winter. My Daddy used to tell us, "Eat what you can, and can what you can't." Nothing ever tasted as good as vegetables grown on this farm.

Some say those who grew up in the mountains experienced cruel childhoods due to poverty and work. I thought it an interesting, busy and imaginative childhood. I loved to see my daddy put the netted hood over his head, put on large thick gloves over a long sleeve shirt and pants and pick up his smoker as he strode into the orchards to steal the honey from the bees. I would stand a long way away, next to the tree, close to the pond in the spot we scouted out for me one day and watch him as he walked up to the hives. I couldn't hear him from that distance, but I knew he sang and talked to his bees. He sang them a lullaby as he pumped in the smoke and reached in gingerly to get the honeycombs out to put in the large silver pan, then added the sticky honey to the top. He would take this in to my Momma, who would strain out the dead bees and fill quart jars with comb and honey. Then they would make a trip into town to trade honey, beeswax candles, sometimes some ginseng or extra produce from the garden and eggs for flour and sugar, maybe if our luck held, pasta or candy. Or they would take a box to the miller when he ground the corn down into meal. They traded a great deal for what they wanted in town, it was the only way, really, to obtain their needs in the poverty ridden town.

They never accepted charity and turned their noses up at the "Commodity Food" that outsiders would bring into the ridge with boxes of half rotted cabbage heads and a pseudo meat patty they called hamburger but sure didn't taste like any hamburger we'd ever had and a square block of bright orange cheese. Daddy always said, "That food's good for nary body, mind nor soul. Accepting charity shrivels up something in a man," he'd say, and he'd point out the Wilson family. "They used to be a good, hard-working family with a nice sized farm and freedom from the gover'ment. Then old man Drake accepted the first welfare check. Ever' since then, all they've thought about was how to get more of that 'free money'. They don't work no more, the only thing they grow is pot, and they have started not even looking like the rest of us. They age faster than most of us and their women are fat and lazy, only worried about chewing their snuff and pushing out babies to get more money on their check. Trust me Lavi (He was the only one who called me that) it just ain't right to take money from the gover'ment, they take your soul in return." He and his like-minded friends called those men, "Happy Pappies."

I remembered a time when Daddy came into the house after working hard all day. His shirt back sopped wet with sweat and he cleaned a long scratch on his arm. He told us, "My day started out bad and just got worse and worse. Sug (his horse) stepped on my foot and I dropped one of the tools for the hay mower and spent hours looking for it in the long grass but I never found the damn thing. I had to leave the field and drive into town to get the part at the Hardware Store. While I waited in line, I bought a Coke (a rare luxury). I was trying to enjoy that and get my perspective back when Drake Jr walked up and opened his fat mouth."

'You know, Callaway, you ain't got to work this hard. All you got do is sign up for the welfare. Me and my boys did and we get all we want and never have to work a lick.' To top it all off, Jr had a case of Ale 8 in one hand and a grocery sack filled with Twinkies and cigarettes in the other. It just made me so mad, here I was feeling guilty about buying a dang coke and he has a sack full of groceries I helped pay for!

I just looked at him and said, 'The Bible says a man will earn his living by the sweat of his brow. I don't want none of that charity money, I want to live free.'" He shook his head, still in disgust about the conversation. "Then if he didn't just keep on talking. That man ain't got the sense God gave a Goose, I swear. He told me, 'Then you are a fool, buddy, a gol darn fool. Everbody 'round here is agin the wall and you're all high and mighty. Think yore better than everbody else, guess you always have even back in school. We laugh at you, slaving away while we do what we want and make our money the easy way.'

Well, I looked him up one side and down the other, I noticed the way his belly was hanging over his pants, he's bow legged, and wrinkled and his skin looks like grey cigarette smoke what teeth he has are black and missing and that long nasty-ass beard of his had crumbs and stuff in it. I just told him, 'We'll see who the fool is, Jr, we'll see.'

And we did see, when Daddy turned sixty-five, he still worked and played hard. His muscles bunched in his arms and he could keep up with his grandkids and nieces and nephews.

He even out ran a niece on the track team on a dare, picked her up and carried her on his back to the house. Jr, on the other hand, could barely walk anywhere. He needed oxygen frequently and just couldn't stay well. I only once heard my daddy come close to an "I told you so," when he saw Drake sitting on a bench next to the post office huffing and struggling to draw in air. Daddy looked at me and said, "That's what using the gover'ment will do. They send bad food and encourage bad ways and we die young. His wife is younger than your momma, but she's in and out of the hospital all the time. Their kids live next door to them, all piled into broken down trailers with grandkids spilling out all of them claiming their backs hurt and getting disability. I've seen 'em climbing a pole and stealing electricity. They got a weird way of living, all on top of each other. Ain't none of 'em happy. They fight amongst themselves and got almost a wolf's way of protecting their pack. They all come in and give their money to the ol woman and she decides who gets to keep what and what they're gonna buy. They share their cars, their trailers and their clothes. Most of the ones they marry find their way out after a while. It's never pretty to watch that. Yore friend from school? Ah, Rick I think his name was. He married the prettiest one out of all them women. She was a looker back then. We talked to him, a bunch of us tried to sit him down and talk to him, but you know how young'uns can be, he wouldn't listen. He just knew he could save her from her ways.

He got that girl pregnant and took her to the preacher. Even the preacher pulled him aside and tried to talk him out of it. Think a man would listen to the preacher huh? Anyway, long story short, they made his life a living hell. He didn't want to live in that trailer with all those people, he tried to get them an apartment. He applied to college wanted her to get her GED, see, he was going to change her. But, you can't change who a person is on the inside. They got in a big fight and she called her Mom and sisters. They came out and packed up everything and took her back to that trailer she loved. She had that baby. Handsome young feller, looked like his dad. But they kept him from his daddy, taught him to hate. That young man is still messed up, always up on dope and booze. I blame it all on a system that teaches people they ain't gotta work and they still get money."

After teaching as long as I have, I figured out what he meant when he said that accepting charity stole the soul of people. Sure, the system remains a godsend for the people who need help. The widows with children, the disabled, the people who fell on hard times and need a helping hand until they get more education, or a better job, they need it and should use it. These people paid into the system, or will pay into the system. They find it an embarrassment to ask, but need to feed their children. But, I've also seen the flip side of that coin, the welfare cycle families. The ones who raise their children to believe that our government owes them something. I tried to teach these children in school, they remained unmotivated, unwilling to learn or better themselves because they knew that a check came in the mail when they said their back hurt or whatever, smart ones always found the loopholes. To me, their eyes look soulless and

59

empty as if they simply wait out their time here on earth and take take take take.

I think it is the giving that makes a person human –the giving of time and money and effort and love. Yes, these families do love each other, but they squabble and engage in drama with each other simply because they are bored. And they raise a bored and entitled next generation. These children form gangs, do drugs, get into trouble.

But, that one child reached makes a difference. That one person who rose out ofthe binds of the cycle. That child makes it worthwhile to teach. I kept in touch throughout the years with a girl from a family like that, Helen. To watch her study and apply to college, get a job, marry a fine young man gives me great joy. I know her greatest trials have been when her family comes to her with hands outstretched, asking her to pay their bills, give her money for this and that, or a drive here or there. Of course, it was hard for her to cut some of the ties and keep others intact. She loves them, but she can't solve their problems. She brought me pictures the other day. She and her new baby mostly, but there was one in which both of her parents were with her and holding the baby. I could see her eyes sparkle with the joy of life and living. Her mother and father's eyes were flat and lifeless – soulless. My dad was right. He usually was.

CHAPTER FOUR:

The rain began to splat on the hood of the car and I rushed to raise the roof and then drove the rest of the way up the drive. When I parked in front of the old yellow station wagon, I saw them standing on the porch – my beautiful mother and her surrogate mother, Honey. I ran up the porch with my bag in my hand to receive two long hugs and I felt at home. Here was the place I longed for in the middle of the night, here was the place of comfort and acceptance that did not depend on what I had cooked for dinner, or cleaned the day before, or accomplished off of someone's mental expectation list. They drew me into the doors, out of the rain, and into a world of my own.

Later that night, after a meal of green beans canned fresh from the garden with large chunks of country ham, sliced tomatoes and cucumber salad, I went to what had always been my room. I put my clothes away in the battered white dresser, then lay down upon the wedding ring quilt in reds and navy blues that covered the mattress of the white iron bed. This room always served as my sanctuary. Much like Emily's, I guess. I could see myself in the room. Instead of Barbies, though, I played with dolls and an old wooden dollhouse crowded with the furniture my dad would carve for me for my birthday or Christmas. The house stood at the foot of the bed on the trunk with its furniture neatly placed inside, waiting for a little girl to love and treasure it. Emily always preferred the new and bright, so she only had interest in it when it was the only thing she had to play with on long weekend visits. Beside the bed stood a desk I used to call my vanity. With only one bathroom and three children trying to get ready at once, I couldn't use the bathroom to do my hair and make-up.

One Saturday afternoon right after I turned thirteen, Daddy and I went to the flea market and bought the desk. With two large

63

drawers on the left side and a long narrow one in the middle the bottom drawer, we thought it held enough space to store my hair stuff: hot rollers, curling iron, hairspray, banana clips and so forth. The top drawer held my make up. In the middle drawer I kept my pens and pencils and school supplies. We painted the desk a bright white, then took all different colors of paint and threw them at the desk – in the 80's we called it splatter painting. We got so much paint on each other that we matched the desk. He carried it into my room and fixed an old mirror above it. For Christmas that year, Momma took an old piano bench and painted it white to match, then made a cushion on the top using a pattern that mimicked the paint colors. I used the space beneath the cushion to hide my diary and love notes, and much later on, my birth control pills. I could still see the slight pink stain on the old cream carpet where Patti dropped my rouge during a slumber party. It had been a magical room at times, and always just mine.

I picked up my cell phone and called Steve to let him know I arrived safely. After our usual conversation of long pauses and awkward questions, we hung up. I laid there and listened to the sound of the rain as it pattered gently upon the tin roof and wondered about where my life was headed and where it had been.

~~~~~~

I was a child. My hair hung in long stringy strands, tangled from the day's adventures. I fed the chickens and got the eggs, boy are they nasty! Then I helped Momma make breakfast for the workers, then I made my bed and swept my room with the broom Daddy made for me that was just my size. Then, Momma said I could go play. I grabbed my bike and rode up and down the drive for a while, until a humongous black snake slithered out of the bushes in front of me and crossed the drive. Daddy said they wouldn't hurt me, but I wasn't going to take any chances! I went to the barn and searched for the new kittens, their momma was a smart one, I could hear them but not find them, then I went on the day's adventures. Eventually, the light started fading and I headed home. I was hungry and tired and just wanted my momma's attention. I went into the kitchen where she was cooking, it was hot in there! She was getting ready to put something into the big black skillet she said Grandma Thompson gave her when she got married, it was spitting and hissing as she dipped some kind of meat from egg to flour and back again.

"Momma, let's go for a walk!" I shout excitedly.

"Not now, Lavani, I've got to get dinner made. Maybe later."

"Momma, you always say that and we NEVER get to it later!"

I pouted and slammed the screen door behind me, walked over to my bike and kicked the wheel. I turned around and could see my mother through the window. She turned around and grabbed something from the icebox, wow was she getting a big belly. Then she reached over and pushed the iron skillet to the back burner of the stove and stepped outside on the porch. Oh man, now I'm in trouble. My lips were already quivering as I looked up at her.

"Come here, Lavani," she said rather crossly. I dragged my feet up the stairs dreading the scolding, I was sure was coming. She handed me a gingersnap cookie and a small glass of milk instead. "Here you go, Baby. You forgot to come in for lunch again." She ruffled the top of my hair as I ate the cookie and drank the milk. I felt better inside, not as empty and gnawing. As I chewed the last bite, I looked up at her quickly. She was staring at me so intently that I thought maybe I was in trouble again.

"Momma?" I questioned.

She started a little, then smiled at me. I relaxed, Momma didn't smile when she was mad. "You know what, Baby, I've been cooped up in the house all day long cleaning and cooking and soon I won't be able to get around much," she patted her giant belly, 'so let's go for that walk right now.'

We walked down the lane. I don't remember what we talked about, but I'm sure I did most of it. We found a thicket of blackberries, just off the side of the drive and I went in and picked us a whole bunch of the sweet berries. I brought her out a handful, she laughed and took them out of my hand and ate them. Then, she wiped the sides of my mouth and teased me about growing a purple mustache. I ran ahead of her and stopped to pick dandelions and purple flowers and brought her back a handful of those too. After she exclaimed over their beauty and how thankful she was, to my grinning delight, she tucked a dandelion behind my ear, then one behind hers. We were giggling and talking when we turned back towards the house. My legs were so tired and achy, I knew I couldn't walk all that way back. I stopped to look at her, and she reached down and picked me up. She set me on her hip, but my legs couldn't reach around her. "Momma, why are you so fat?"

She laughed, "It's because of the baby that's in there. And, if I'm right with my bet, I'd say it's more like babies!" She laughed again. I loved the sound of her voice and her laughter and laid my head on her shoulder and smelled her neck. Every now and then, I would just kiss her right there on the neck, as she walked us home. She smelled like Momma, kind of spicy, yet sweet. She reminded me of the jasmine that grew in the garden and how it mixed with the vanilla smells from the kitchen, when Momma was baking.

A few minutes later, we heard the sound of my daddy's old Chevy truck behind us. Momma turned with a giant smile on her face and her eyes had that sparkly look they got when Daddy was around. "Hey there, that's two beautiful ladies on the road, are you headed my way?"

I giggled, "Daddy, it's us!"

"Why, so it is! I didn't know you under all that dirt and purple mustache!" He got out of the truck and I jumped into his arms. "Hello, Gorgeous" he said as he leaned over to kiss Momma right on the mouth! Momma walked to the other side of the truck, while Daddy put me into the middle. "What's for dinner?" he asked as she shut the door.

She laughed again when I held up her flowers and opened my fist where two berries were squished between my fingers, "Berries and flowers!!"

He rolled his eyes and hit the gas when she repeated, "Berries and flowers!"

~~~~~~
~~~~~~~~~~~~~~~~

I awoke to the easing of the rain on the roof, covered with a light afghan and the light off. Smiling at the dream memory, and being taken care of, I fell back asleep. Berries and flowers, indeed.

Truth and Grace

CHAPTER FIVE:

The next morning, the chimes from my cell phone woke me at 4:00, time to get the day started. I dressed comfortably and walked into the kitchen. Honey, already up, handed me a full cup of coffee. "Honey, you don't have to take care of me, I'm here to take care of you two!" I kissed her on the cheek in lieu of thanks.

"And thanks for covering me up last night, I felt just like a child."

She laughed in that infectious little girl giggle of hers, it sounded so incongruous coming from an elderly lady, "Child, if I didn't have someone to take care of, I think I'd die. I've been taking care of people since I was born I think and I will until the day I die, but I'm not the one that covered you, I went to bed and sleep right after you did."

I wrapped my arm around her shoulders and squeezed, noticing for the first time that her sturdy strength had turned into fragility. I looked at her directly in the face, and could see her eyes clouded with a worry she tried not to show. "Honey, I promise I will call and let you know everything as soon as I know. I left my number on the pad by the telephone, you can call me anytime you want."

"Oh, I know that. I just know this is bad. Your momma, now she won't complain, but I got that feeling."

The hair stood up on the back of my neck and cold chills raced through my body. Honey's "feelings" were legendary in my family. She was one of the most intuitive women I've ever known. She'd come in while I was getting ready for a date, "Now, Vani, you have a good time, but I have a feeling that this one has some wild ways. Don't let him get his hands on you, you're a good girl." All that night I'd be fighting his hands off, or hanging onto the 'oh hell handle' while he was driving like a madman. Or, "Vani, this boy's awful sweet, but I have a feeling he's not the one for you." Then I would yawn my way through dinner and a movie and once yawned right in the face of a boy who was trying to kiss me. Talk about embarrassing. Only once she had said to me, "I have a feeling this is the One!" The only other time that her "feeling" had made the hair stand up on the back of my neck like this was when I handed her my newborn son. She cuddled him close and baby talked with him, then with a white face handed him back to me. "Oh, Darling, I have such a bad feeling..." then she quickly left the room and never mentioned her feeling again. But in the months and years that followed, I often thought of her feeling.

"It will be ok, Honey," I gave her another quick squeeze and we both looked up as Momma came into the kitchen.

"Are you all conspiring against me?" she asked with a crooked grin. We all pretended to laugh and finished getting ready for our trip. We needed to be in Lexington by 6:30 for the surgery and the trip took an hour. Momma wanted to get there early, just in case, so we planned to leave by 5:00. I yawned and picked up my travel mug of coffee and announced, "Let's head out!"

Momma looked at my purple sweatsuit, "Oh, are you wearing that?"

My defensiveness immediately kicked in, "Yes, it's comfortable, I'm not going to try to win a fashion competition, you know."

"I just thought you'd try to fix up a little bit. You have such a pretty face, I wish you'd try to play it up some. People who wear sweats just look like they've given up."

In other words, I looked like a fat slob. Great, what a way to start an already stressful day." Let's go," I said between gritted teeth. I took long and deep breaths thinking, 'Out with the negative, in with the positive. Out with anger and hurt and in with love and patience.' Well, sometimes it worked for me.

Honey and Momma hugged for a second, then we left the peace of home behind to the slamming of the screen door. Honey stood on the other side and waved at us until we turned out of sight.

At first we drove in strained silence with some radio talk show murmuring in the background. Momma looked at the scenery and seemed to be taking it all in. Once we swung out onto the interstate, she watched me take a long drink of my now cooling coffee, "Oh how I'm jealous of that coffee," she stated, "I don't think I've not had a cup of coffee in a morning since I was 5 years old and my mom made me some hot milk with lots of sugar and a drop of coffee. I've drank it ever since, only the drops of coffee kept getting bigger and bigger." Her comments broke the ice and we laughed because Momma's love of strong coffee was a family joke. Everyone teased her that we could stand spoons up in her cups of brew. She had her own little coffee pot, and everyone else drank Honey's. "Your daddy, now, he was the only person who ever would sit and drink my coffee with me," she laughed. "I knew it was a forever kind of love when I poured him that first cup the morning after we said our

'I do's' and he drank it and asked for more. What was that commercial when you were young? Oh yeah, 'Fill it to the rim with Brim,' he'd say and we'd laugh and laugh and drink a whole pot between us."

I loved hearing Momma talk about Daddy. She'd get that same sparkly look in her eyes that I remembered from my dream last night. "How old were you when you met Daddy?"

"Oh, five, I think. He said right away he was going to marry me. But I gave him a hard time about it and made him wait almost twenty years. I wanted to wait one more year, but he finally lost his patience and said he was done with me. When I knew I couldn't live without him, I begged and cried and pleaded for him to take me back. He stood there in the doorway with his arms crossed. 'All you had to do was ask,' he said when I finished my begging, then he took me in his arms and kissed me until my toes curled. We went to the courthouse as soon as we got our license and blood work finished."

She smiled at the memory and I did too, it was one of my favorite stories. "Tell me again how you met."

She laughed, "Aren't you tired of that story? Besides your daddy told it better than me."

"Tell me anyway, his version, please." I pleaded.

"OK, you always were a romantic. I will try to tell it the way he always did." she said with a gentle grin.

"It was a rare day of leisure for your dad and he couldn't wait to get it started. He and his best friend went running through the woods and towards their favorite place to play. A house was being built in town and they had dug out a basement leaving a giant pile of dirt in the yard. The workers wouldn't be there since it was Sunday, so they were headed for that first thing. No self-respecting eight year old boy could resist a mountain of dirt!" She exclaimed.

"They raced up the 'mountain' and immediately began to wrestle and try to throw the other one down the side of it, shouting, 'I am King of the Mountain,' but they were pretty evenly matched. His shirt had just gotten torn a little and things were starting to heat up when suddenly a small hand was placed into the middle of his back and he was shoved right off the top of that mountain.

As he and his friend rolled down that hill, he would catch a glimpse of sky then dirt then sky then dirt until he landed in a heap at the bottom. Incredulously he looked to the top, no one had ever beaten the two of them at wrestling, or well, anything. They were just too big and too strong. He wanted to see the big boy that had.

Standing there at the top was the smallest little girl he had ever seen. She had long black hair that flowed softly in the wind and golden skin that glowed in the sun. Her dark brown eyes were lit up with the challenge of defeating two big boys and, with her hands on her hips, she threw her head back and laughed, 'I am QUEEN of the mountain!'

It was in that very instant he felt his heart jump up and knew this was the woman he'd marry and have kids with. In that very instant, while his friend muttered and griped and he could feel the aches of the fall that he knew she'd break his heart but he'd love her anyway. And he gave her his entire heart and his entire being. It was that moment that he vowed to be a good enough man she'd want to marry him some day. At least, that's as close as I can get to the way he used to tell the story," she laughed.

After a few minutes, she muttered, almost to herself, "He liked to say that I saved him. He saved me. Or, rather, I guess we saved each other."

"What do you mean you all saved each other?" I asked, confused by that statement.

"Well, Lavani, neither your dad nor I had an easy childhood, you know. We made ourselves better than we should have been because we loved each other and wanted children. We didn't want our children to have such a hard upbringing, or experience the things either of us experienced in our lives."

"Tell me about your childhoods, Momma, neither one of you would ever talk about them."

"Now is not the time. I want to think about only good things before my surgery. I've always thought, good positive thoughts keep a person as healthy as anything else." She leaned back in her seat and we spoke of our gardens and canning and freezing. I know this sounds kind of crazy, but we finally began to bond a few years back over our love of preserving things from the garden and we both loved to cook. Well, I used to love to cook. I had even thought at one time about changing careers and going to culinary school. But, then things happened and I got older and it became easier to do what I had always done. I mean, I think I am a good teacher. My students like me and I get good observation scores, from my peers and principals. I've outlived three statewide school reforms, three different kinds of testing and "No Child Left Behind," and that's quite an accomplishment.

Teachers my age were anymore, just too much change and not enough recognition or pay. Had Steve not obtained such a good job, I could not have taught. But the hours and days of teaching suited a family life, so we both decided he would work overtime as needed and I would be a teacher. And a housekeeper. And a chauffeur. And a nurse. And a cook. And a gardener. And well, anything that needed to be done. It was just a typical life of a Mom and I wouldn't take back any moment of any time spent with my children.

I did have one regret, in my teaching career. I left the high school for a while because of the needs of my children. To bring in a little money, one of the ladies I went to church with helped me get a job at the local community college. I loved that job. Probably too much. I taught as adjunct faculty for a while and then they hired me full time. I knew my strength as a teacher shone at the college level, my students loved me, I received great reviews from the Deans and my supervisors. I thought I would stay there until I retired. Then, life happened.

I was diagnosed with Cervical Cancer. My initial surgery went bad and led to over twenty surgeries in five years. I eventually lost a kidney and part of my bladder. I missed a great deal of work, between my own health and that of my son's. Then, Christian became worse and then worse yet. He suffered from Cystic Fibrosis, that is the terrible feeling Honey had and during this time in our lives, he also developed Diabetes. The doctors began to talk to us about setting up his "Make a Wish" while he felt strong enough to enjoy it. CF is a terrible disease. It affects all parts of the body, except the brain. It also demands a great deal from the caregiver. I stayed up most nights with him as he coughed and his sugar went up and down, dealt with my own illness and stress and still taught. I thought I balanced it well. I developed a class that focused purely upon service learning, the fad at the time, and I felt like Superwoman. The Academic Dean complimented me one day and asked me to help him set up a service learning project in his class. Then a week later, my supervisor called me in to a meeting.

To make a long story short, they fired me. Apparently, when I became sick my direct supervisor (one I wrongly considered a friend) began keeping detailed notes about my actions and location at all times. If she did not find me in my office during my office hours, she documented it – of course she didn't notate that I was in the library helping a student, or attending a meeting with one of the clubs I voluntarily sponsored, or in the bathroom. Then, she trumped up false charges based on one student's complaints. A student who missed seven of sixteen classes couldn't believe her grade and filed a complaint that I didn't grade her work. She didn't turn in her work and I didn't accept late work. I appealed in a long drawn out process, but of course lost the appeal with the "judges" being people the Dean picked. I consulted a lawyer who advised me to fight fight fight, but I didn't have the fight left in me anymore.

The day they fired me, I gathered my things from my office, then threw the key on my former friend's desk. I just knew all my friends and colleagues would support me, there would be throngs of students protesting in my name. Not one. Not one of my colleagues stood for me. In fact, several of them testified against me. One, a special confidante, who spent two years crying on my shoulder about her son's time in prison, wrote a letter of complaint about me. Another said I used my son's illness as an "excuse" to not do anything. I volunteered every year to help her with her back to school orientation. I did everything from bake cookies to teach a seminar, it wasn't enough. Even my very best friend there didn't help me. She "forgot" to write the letter she promised. She was just too busy. I resented them – all of them. I knew that for my own good, I needed to let it go, but even driving past the building still caused me to feel anger and nausea.

Several of my students did stand for me. They testified for me, brought papers I graded, wrote letters and, honestly, restored some of my faith in other people. The day I decided that I could not fight anymore, I found myself home alone – the kids in school, Steve at work. I sat on the porch that day, drinking coffee and feeling useless. The night before we signed up for Steve's medical and life insurance there was no clause about suicide canceling the benefits. I rocked in my chair on the porch and thought about getting my pistol and going in the house and just shooting myself in the head. I reasoned I was worth more dead than alive. No one would really care except my children and they were young, they would get over it. Steve would probably remarry and anyone he chose would be better than me.

I had it planned. I would get everything ready first. I didn't want anyone to have to clean up after me too much, so I would lay a sheet in the bathtub, then climb in and pull the curtain closed. Then, I would call my friend who is a policeman and tell him that I left the door unlocked, please send someone to find me so that my family wouldn't. Then, I would hang up, lie down and shoot myself before anyone could get there. I even researched the best place to put the bullet to ensure it would work.

I teetered there on the edge for a long time. Then, a friend called me. She just wanted to tell me she loved me and thought about me. It made a difference to me, someone somewhere cared about me. I got up, walked into the house, put my pistol in the gun cabinet and locked it, I never could remember the combination. It stayed there for several years until I trusted myself. I found a new strength that day. I decided to let the anger and hatred go, it only hurt me. Those people never cared about me, they never thought about me; the only person I hurt was me. I discovered which "friends" would stand for me, and which would not. I honestly was surprised by some that did, and very very grateful. Mostly, though, I came to find out I could be strong through a crisis. There was more to me than even I knew.

Probably, losing that job turned out to be a blessing. My son became too sick for me to work so I stayed with him, both at home and at the hospital. We enjoyed a very close relationship during that time. His health continued to decline but I positively knew for sure a miracle would save him. God could never let my son die. He would never abandon such a great kid. I demonstrated strength and He would reward that strength with my son's healing.

Arrogance like that, never goes unpunished. I discovered what would put me right back on that porch weak and frightened and hurting way more, than losing a job.

Truth and Grace

Truth and Grace

CHAPTER SIX:

I could not have been thinking any worse possible thoughts when we pulled into the parking garage at UK hospital and around until we found a good parking spot. I knew this hospital like the back of my hand. Before I got out of the car, I stopped and took a deep breath. I felt those little shivers of panic racing from my suddenly numb teeth down my back and back up into my stomach. I became queasy, started seeing spots, my chest tightened until I felt like I couldn't draw in a breath. Momma's voice came from far away, "Lavani? Lavani? Are you alright?"

I fought to get past the anxiety and used some tricks my grief counselor had taught me until finally I could see clearly and breathe fully. "Oh, Lavani, I'm so sorry I asked you to bring me, I didn't even think about you being here and how that would make you feel." Her brown eyes shone with tears as she stroked my hair and I realized I had my door open and was leaning out with my head between my knees. Her voice sounded soft and shaky, and I knew she was upset too.

"Momma,it's fine. I'm fine. I wanted to bring you, let's go." I couldn't help being a little gruff with her. I knew if I stopped and tried to be nice, I'd start crying and neither one of us needed that. Besides, I've always been afraid that one day I would start crying and not be able to stop. For the rest of my life, and I prayed it would be short, I would sob when I talked and tears would run down my face and make everyone run away from me. So, I just couldn't chance that this might be the time that happened, I choked down the tears and the anxiety then grabbed the suitcase from the back of the car. We set off down the walkway over the road and into the lobby of the hospital.

As soon as we reached the lobby, we heard a familiar whistle, "Hey there pretty ladies, going our way?"

We looked over to see my grinning "little" brother and his twin, my gorgeous sister. They ran to us and grabbed us and held us a few minutes. We all talked at the same time until finally our momma said, "How did you know?"

Jay answered, "Well, Vani called us. You should have told us, Momma. We want to be here for you!" With his thick black hair slightly too long to be stylish, and his dark glasses that covered his green eyes, he looked almost exactly like my daddy. At 40, he was a little thicker than he used to be, but in good shape, especially for someone who lived in his office or the sanctuary of his church most of the time. But, I knew he and his family biked together and hiked together quite a bit. He waited until later in life to marry and married a younger woman we all adored and his kids were quite a bit younger than mine.

His twin, my baby sister, stood beside me smiling with her arm around my waist. She had been my baby growing up. Momma teased that I mothered her more than she did. Jayce (yes my parents fell into that pattern of naming them alike) kissed Momma's cheek. Her subtle perfume enveloped us. At 40 she still looked like a model. She modeled from the time she turned fifteen and talent scouts "discovered" her at the mall, until she graduated from college. It paid for her education. After she graduated with her law degree, she made it clear she'd never take pictures for a living again. She stayed slender after four babies, but curvy in all the right spots and innately knew how to wear clothes. She pulled her hair into a loose French braid that lay over her shoulder and highlighted her almond shaped green eyes. With high cheekbones and golden skin, her appearance combined everything good about my parents.

At a much younger time, we treated ourselves by watching the movie Arnold Schwarzenegger and Danny DeVito starred in, *Twins*. In the movie, scientists created a perfect child with the DNA of several different men (Arnold's character). After his birth, they

94

discovered an unexpected twin who inherited all the bad traits of the men (Danny's character). Since we saw that movie, I felt like Danny's character. My little brother and sister possessed all the grace and talent and good looks and I got stuck with the leftoers. But, at least I didn't have a name like Jay and Jayce.

I felt frumpy and kind of stupid when I compared myself to them. I looked at my sister's perfectly pressed long white pants, worn with a teal short sleeve v-neck shirt and her gold colored sandals. She carried a coordinating jacket in a slightly darker shade of teal. Her accessories stood out, a chunky gold necklace, a slim gold bracelet and short dangling earrings. She perfectly applied her make-up and her hair looked effortless. I knew she had gotten up that morning and made breakfast for her kids and husband before she drove the hour, to the hospital. I, on the other hand, stood a little less than five feet tall and carried forty pounds too many. I wore the sweat suit my mother complained about (probably out of spite) and just pulled my shoulder length salt and pepper hair off my face with a barrette and a ponytail holder. I didn't wear make-up often and my plain hazel eyes faded without mascara. I felt hot red blotches on my cheeks and nose from my panic attack earlier. My mother stood between us in her fairy like glory. She wore her completely white hair styled in a shoulder length bob, even for surgery she had applied a little bit of base, mascara and lipstick. She dressed in gray pants and a white button up shirt that emphasized her tiny waist. She wore black flats and a silver chain necklace and her wedding band. Jayce certainly got her style from our mother.

We all shuffled into the pre-surgery waiting room and just talked quietly about kids and spouses and normal activities. Momma listened intently, a little quieter than usual until they called her name, "Sarah Thompson." Suddenly, she looked nervous for the first time. Her hand gripped mine with surprising strength as she breathed deeply then stood up.

"Follow me, please, Ma'am," the young and just slightly annoyingly, too perky nurse said. I followed them as well, while Jay and Jayce stayed seated until called. It was just understood that when it came to doctors and medical situations, I knew more and did better than they.

We went back into the pre-op area where Momma changed her clothes and put them in the large blue surgery bag. The nurse came in as Momma gave me her necklace to keep for her, "Your ring needs to go, too," she said.

"But, I never take this off. I've had it on for over fifty years," Momma protested.

"I'm sorry, Ma'am, but if you don't take it off, we will have to remove it during surgery and you don't want it to be lost or damaged. I'm sure your sister here will take care of it."

Daughter," I said, hating this young thing.

"Of course, now just give it to her and I will get your IV placed and we can get this show on the road, Mrs Thompson."

It took a few minutes to work the ring over Momma's knuckles, but we got it off and I slid the plain white gold band over her silver necklace then fastened it around my neck. "Don't worry, Momma, as soon as you are out of surgery, I will put it back on your hand where it belongs."

We looked at her hand. They were wrinkled with age, but still rather long and slim. She kept her nails short and neat and painted a natural glossy color. The third finger of her left hand had a deep white indention where her ring should have been and she keep rubbing the spot with her other hand, much like someone does with their tongue when there is a chipped tooth in their mouth.

The nurse came in and did the IV, thankfully it only took one try and hooked her up to a saline drip. She talked cheerfully all the while, but she talked to my mother as she would a child. I kept waiting for Momma to correct her, to tell her she had earned a degree more advanced than the nurse did, but she never said anything. She just answered the questions. "Now, the doctor will be here in just a minute. Is there anyone else you would like to see before surgery? Do you need to pee-pee?"

I winced at the tone of voice and word choice from the nurse, but Momma just answered, "Yes, please. Do you mind getting my other daughter and son from the waiting room? I'd like them to sit with me, too."

While the nurse was gone, we remained silent, each thinking our own thoughts until my sister and brother slipped quietly into the room. My brother settled on the end of bed and my sister sat in the other chair and we talked quietly and waited for all the pre surgery routine to be over. First, the anesthesiologist came in to make sure Momma knew what would happen as he put her to sleep and what medications she took. "Mrs. Thompson, anytime you get nervous you just ask and I have a medicine that will help you." He went on to explain what pain medication she would be on after the surgery. "Any questions?"

"No, I think I'm fine," she answered.

"OK, I will see you in there, unless you need me first." The doctor replied.

"Momma, feel free to go on and use the medication," my sister said.

"No, not yet," I interrupted, "She will want to talk to her doctor first. Then, I would say night night."

"Good thinking," my brother said and reached for Momma's hand. "Momma, let's say a prayer together."

We each bowed our heads, as Jay asked the Lord to watch over Momma during the surgery and to guide the surgeon's hands and yadda yadda yadda. My brother was a preacher at one of the largest churches in Louisville. I heard him preach many times, and knew he preached well, but I also knew he lived what he preached. He and his wife excelled as faithful Christians, and raised their children to be the same. He prayed earnestly and heartfelt, but I didn't close my eyes. I quit praying years ago.

God and I, well we had a live and let live kind of relationship going. For the last five years, it had been like this. I went to church to keep up appearances, but there did not experience a real prayer or meditation time in my heart. I felt too, well I guess the word would be, betrayed by God. My grief counselor said I had to forgive Him, but I thought that sounded arrogant, and frankly, impossible, certainly not something, I wanted to try.

I think my questions were generic, but still deeply concerning. Why did God allow all these assholes and jerks to live and take the young and the good? I kept thinking, if I knew someone was going to come into the classroom with a gun and shoot everyone, and I had the power to stop it, but didn't; then, I would be as guilty as the person who did the shooting. I would be an accomplice. I always believed that God knew everything and could do anything, so why did he allow so many bad things to happen? Why did he let a man walk into a school and shoot all the children and teachers? Why did he let car accidents maim and kill? Why did he let nasty men molest children? Why did he not cure the sick and dying even when entire towns were praying? What kind of God allows that to happen? He could strike any of them at any time with a bolt of lightning. He could say one word and all the sick children would be healed. Yet, he didn't. In my mind, a God worth worshiping would protect his people. He would heal the sick, raise the dead and make the blind see and the lame to walk. But, this line of questioning made too many people uncomfortable, and really, no one had the answers. So, in church, I just bowed my head but refused to close my eyes in defiance to this God.

My brother tried to talk to me, he told me all about free will and the consequences of the original sin. He talked about Heaven and infinity and the limited time we knew on this earth. I didn't want to hear it; I would nod until he figured out I only humored him, then I would change the subject. My parents raised me to love God, and I'm not sure I ever stopped, but I found I could not trust Him nor respect Him.

After the prayer, we continued to hold hands until another doctor stepped into the room. This one, with his trendy haircut and Converse sneakers, half shaved face and bored eyes looked like a young and sulky teenager. "Good morning, Mrs. Thompson, how are you today?"

Without waiting for her answer he slid right into his prepared speech "Today you will have a surgery. First, we will enter vaginally and take a biopsy, then we send it to the lab. At that point, we will wait to hear back from the lab; if it comes back cancerous, we will do what is called a 'radical hysterectomy.' This is a procedure in which we will remove both ovaries, both fallopian tubes, your uterus and cervix and part of your vaginal wall. We will also remove any close lymph nodes. At that time we will know what stage cancer you are in." His voice was almost monotone, disinterested in this operation.

"After the surgery, you will have some pain and discomfort, but we will make sure that you have adequate pain medication available." He droned on and on about possible side effects or complications from the surgery, then had my mother sign her permission to treat. "Good luck, I'll see you in the operating room soon." And he turned and tried to leave.

"Wait!," I stopped him. "I have some questions."

He sighed heavily as he turned around, as if I bothered him, "Yes?" he replied in a faraway disinterested voice, looking like that sulky spoiled teen who wanted to be somewhere way more cool than here.

"First, I understood my mother's doctor was Dr. Rose. Where is she today?"

"She will be in presently, but I've told you all you need to know."

Great, a defensive one, I thought. "When you say 'we will do the surgery' that means she will do it and you will observe, right?"

"Ma'am I am fully trained to do the surgery at this point." he shot back.

"I understand that, but I want to make sure my mother has the doctor she is comfortable with and has contracted with, to perform this surgery." I snapped.

Red color surged into his face. "She will be here soon," and he turned on his heel and left without another backwards glance.

"Little asshole twerp," I muttered under my breath.

"Momma, have you met him before? He's terrible!"

"Now, Lavani, he's alright. He's a surgeon, we have to give him some leeway."

"No, you don't. You deserve a surgeon and a doctor who is good and kind and caring. I know they have them here. You don't deserve someone who treats you so coldly, especially when you are going through so much!"

"Lavani," she said rather sharply, "I'm not a child, you don't have to fight your famous battles over me. This isn't about you." Removing her hand from mine and turning to face the other side, she said, "I'm ready for that medication."

The nurse came in and put it through her IV line, her pretty eyes closed and she softly fell asleep. The nurses came to get her and rolled her out of the pre-op room into the operating room, leaving us to make our way to the waiting room.

As we left the room, I wondered how many times I walked away from a loved one being wheeled in the opposite direction; how many hours I spent waiting on doctors in waiting rooms, hospital rooms, and clinics; how many times I said sgood-bye to the ones I loved most in the world. Feeling sick, I laid my forehead against the coolness of the concrete wall. I focused on deep breathing and positive imagery until I could raise my head and face the sympathetic faces of my brother and sister. Jayce grabbed my hand and we left the hallway holding hands.

Truth and Grace

CHAPTER SEVEN:

Always the peace maker, Jayce squeezed my hand as we entered the waiting room, "She didn't mean to be short with you, Vani, she's just upset and nervous."

"I know. I didn't take it personally," but we both knew I did. We went down the hall from the waiting room into the crowded cafeteria for some breakfast. I wondered how many times I had eaten food from that place in my lifetime as I put another cup of coffee on my tray with some gravy and biscuits. Jay chose the same thing and Jayce grabbed a yogurt and some fresh fruit. They both drank coffee as well. We ate slowly, the hospital had given us a "buzzer" that would light up with red lights and make a noise if they needed us back in the waiting room.

As we ate we talked of the things brothers and sisters do, our jobs and children, our spouses. I didn't have much to say, I mean really what could I add? "I think Emily is OK and Steve is an ass. I miss my son so much it hurts

and it doesn't get any better as time goes on"
They already knew how Emily loved being in
New York and pursuing her dream. And they
already knew Steve was an ass, neither liked
him, they hadn't for a long time. And they hurt
with losing Christian as well.

After we finished our meal and returned
to the waiting room, we sat nervously. I flipped
through a recent issue of *Good Housekeeping,*
restlessly until the attendant at the desk
announced over the loudspeaker that the
Thompson family needed to report to Consulting
Room number 1.

Once we entered, we waited a couple of
minutes until the surgeon came in. I knew by the
look on her face she had bad news.

"We were able to get the biopsy vaginally
and sent it to the lab. There was definitely
cancer present. We went on and opened her to
begin the radical hysterectomy, but I'm going to
tell you it's not good news. She is at least Stage
III, possibly Stage IV. There is a great deal of
damage present, the tumor was large and not

contained. I'm sorry. I'm going to go back and finish the hysterectomy, my resident will keep you updated from time to time. I anticipate this surgery will last about four hours, possibly more." Her voice was warm, even as she gave us such bad news. Her gray eyes regarded us each with compassion. "After she is finished with the surgery, I am going to send her to the ICU for a couple of days. I want to keep her on the ventilator and let her completely rest for at least 24 hours. I'm worried that this surgery will be very hard on her because of her age. You will be allowed to see her briefly in the Recovery Room, but I recommend that you make it a quick visit and then get some rest. You are going to need it to help her when she leaves this place. She is going to be incredibly sore and weak due to blood loss and the incision pain as well as the pelvic pain. Do you have any questions for me?"

We couldn't think of a single question.

The first night I slept in the room with Momma, I couldn't sleep. I thought about a conversation I had taken part in on Facebook as a friend tried to deal with the loss of her beautiful mother because of cancer. Tara posted, "This damn disease needs a different name. Every time its name is said, I just feel like it has power. Its name doesn't do it justice. Its name is too benign. 'Insidious' is too cool for it. It needs a name that belittles it, that diminishes its power. It is a parasite. And yes I know we learn messages because of its existence. And yes I know positive things come from our experience with it. But, every time its name is said there is a battle beginning or continuing. It uses our fears against us. The F-Word is a powerful word. Calling the C-Word empowers it. We need to disparage it. It sneaks in and tortures those we love and sometimes takes them from us. It is a coward."

What could it be called instead? I struggled to find the right word. There is not one that encompasses the fear, the hate, the pain associated with cancer. After surviving it myself, and finding out Momma would be fighting the same battle, I felt weary at the

113

beginning of this fight. I posted to her, "Sometimes, it's just too much to handle. We learn from it, yes, but not enough – not ever enough for the price we pay." I wished I offered her words of comfort or enlightenment, I wished I possessed them. I only gave her sympathy. From talking to the doctors today, I realized, the word meant the battle neither began nor continued with Momma; rather, it meant the battle ended.

Later that week my friend's post made me laugh. She and another friend came up with the perfect name! "…dingleberry! It implies some sort of mass but it greatly reduces its 'ominence' factor. If Mom had known she had dingleberry, she would have laughed so hard that snot came out of her nose!" I read this to my momma while we talked one day waiting to be released and she laughed so hard she cried. So did I.

I stayed with Momma the week the doctors kept her at the hospital. I slept on a fold back recliner in her room and helped wherever I could. I ran to get her the food she thought would taste good and helped hold her as she walked around the hallways. We talked some and laughed some and she slept while I read or made lists of things I needed to do. It reminded me of all the times I spent there with Christian.

I saw him in every hallway, it seemed. I dreamed of him at night. His presence surrounded me even more than usual. I even visited the children's hospital and talked to some of his old nurses. They remembered him, and me, and I caught them up with Emily's life and my own. Those nurses, at one time, were my family. They even brought us dinner when Christian lay so sick. I loved them as I loved my sister and brother. When Christian's visitation and funeral were over, I counted the names of the ones who signed in, and over seventy attended. They loved him, and he loved them.

At first, I thought it would be devastating to be there again. But, in a way, it also resolved some of my emotions. I wrapped up some of the loose ends of the relationships suddenly severed.

115

I found out Dee would soon be a grandmother, David taught nursing classes, Karen won big in the lottery. Melissa and Brian were still best friends and poor Julie died in a car wreck. Donna and Ruth Anne retired and Ruth Anne lived in Disney while Donna travelled the United States in her RV with her husband. Bridget and Katie worked in the NICU full time now and Stacie ran the entire floor. I couldn't believe how much Wyatt, her son, had grown. Leneigha and Trinaye were married with children. And Michael Anne was crazily in love with her new husband. Meg still worked with cancer patients, even though she just had her third child. I didn't realize, until then, what a great impact these amazing nurses made on my life and how, even years later, I felt so incredibly grateful for their roles in my life. Of course, I didn't catch up with all of them, some had quit nursing, or moved on to other facilities, but all of them, all of them changed me for the better.

When the doctors released Momma from the hospital, I felt more at peace than I had in years. "Are you OK, Momma," I asked as I helped her into the car to make the trip home. I handed her a pillow, "I know after I had my C-sections and my surgeries, if I pushed a pillow hard into my stomach when I sneezed or coughed, it really helped. It helps with pot holes and big bumps too. I will try to warn you if I am going to hit something like that."

Momma's eyes were a bit glazed from the pain medication the nurse gave to her right before wheeling her to the car. "Thank you."

We drove in silence for a little while during rush hour as I navigated my way out of traffic and onto the interstate. Once we hit the interstate, I relaxed. I didn't have the top down, but I still loved the smoothness of my car as it sped along the interstate. Momma stayed awake so I commented, "Honey will be so glad to see you. She has called twice a day every day about you. She sure loves you."

She smiled, "She always has, ever since she came to the house to take care of us, we've been best friends.

"Momma, tell me how Honey became your step-momma. It seems like she is so close to your age. I think it's great you all have always loved each other so much." her voice, a little wispy with the medication warmed, as she told me what I'd never known.

"My mother was a full blooded Cherokee Indian, from the mountains. I think my father loved her, but he always seemed embarrassed to be with her. She was beautiful, in the Indian way. Short, but very strong. Long black hair she always wore in a braid, her skin was golden colored and her cheekbones were high. I always thought she had the prettiest brown eyes. They were so deep, like she could see inside my soul and loved what she saw. Her name was Chandrika, in our language that would be, "Moonlight." She gave each of us a Cherokee name as well, mine is Dayita or Beloved. That comforted me after she died. In her language I was beloved."

Momma paused for a long time, I almost thought she had fallen asleep until she continued. "My Momma died giving birth to a stillborn child when I was eleven. I was the oldest of seven children. At first, Father thought I could take care of all of them, but I was just too young and they wouldn't listen to me anyway. After a couple of months of chaos, a dirty house, burned dinners and smelly clothes, not to mention crying children and loud fights I guess he had had enough.

Our neighbors were dirt poor farmers who scrabbled to get by. They had lots of kids, seemed like a new baby every year. Honey was one of the middle children. She had just turned thirteen when Father went to her house. He took her father out in the barn for a discussion. I can just imagine how this talk would go over in this day and time! Anyway, he told Honey's dad that he would give him $500 if he would let Honey marry him and live with us. Father promised he would never touch her "in the Biblical way" until she was at least eighteen, and then only if she agreed. He had seen how Honey was the one who took care of all the kids and the house, such as it was, and he wanted her to come and straighten all of us out, but he was a religious man who didn't want any rumors around town either. That was a fortune in that day and age so Honey's dad went in the house and brought her out with all her 'worldly goods' in a brown paper sack and my dad took her straight to town and married her in front of the Justice of the Peace.

When he came home with Honey, she walked into the kitchen and made a huge supper. It was wonderful! The best meal we had since my momma died. That night, when the rest of them were asleep, I snuck down to the kitchen. She had warmed up several pans of water on the stove and was pouring it into the big washtub. When it was full, she grabbed some of our 'store bought' soap and scrubbed and scrubbed her skin then she sank into the water up to her chin. She stayed like that for so long that I thought she must have fallen asleep. 'Sarah, since you are

120

here, why don't you come help me wash my hair?' she said startling me with her quiet voice. I was a timid little thing, believe it or not, and it took me a few moments to decide, but I walked over and helped her wash her hair out. That water was dirty! I had never seen so much crud in the bottom of the tub. Honey was pink all over, scrawny like me, I'm not even sure she had hit puberty at the time. I ran upstairs and got her one of my long nightgowns and a brush. After she threw out the bathwater, she let me brush her hair in front of the fire, just like my momma always had. Her hair was different, silky where Momma's had been kind of coarse, and a reddish blonde color. It was the prettiest thing about her. She went to sleep in my sister's and my room that night, and every night after. My dad kept his word and never touched her.

During the day while we were at school, she'd clean the house and work in the garden, cooking dinner and doing laundry. At night, we would share our lessons with her. She learned how to read and do math, in fact, she became as educated as us. There wasn't a book she wouldn't devour if it was close to her. But, my very favorite times were when the other kids were in bed, and the house was settled for the night, Father would be snoring in his bedroom, we'd pull out our dolls and play house. Or, as we got older, we'd listen to records and dance or just talk and giggle. Honey became, and still is, my very best friend.

Father was always, well... I think the word would be, distant. It was like he could not actually reach out to us kids. He would watch us, but the only conversation was when he was telling us what to do. He loved us all, but he didn't know how to express that love. Honey filled that void with lots of hugs and kisses and praise. I was too old to be raised by her, but she really made the children's lives more fulfilled and happier as a step mother. She made mine better as a friend.

Father passed away when Honey was 17 ½. She still took care of us and when she remarried, her new husband took care of the kids too. He was a good man. She did laugh though, on their wedding night he was amazed that he'd married a virgin widow! We were girls together, we became women together and now we are old together. I think she saved my life. Honey isn't her real name, by the way. We just have all called her that for so long, that's what she goes by, her real name is Mary."

Momma was quiet for quite a while, I thought she had fallen asleep again. For a few miles I pondered what she had said. What a story! I couldn't wait to tell Jay and Jayce the whole story. "You know, Lavani, yours is an Indian name. Lavani means Grace. Jayce means Strong and Jayant means Victorious. I think I got all the names right on target." I had never heard this story before and was amazed at the meaning of our names.

"How did I become Vani?" I asked.

She chuckled, "Your father thought giving you an Indian name might cause you to have problems in school, so we agreed that you could go by a nickname to the world and Lavani to us, everyone else but me ended up calling you by your nickname. I always call you Lavani because it was by Grace you were given to me. I didn't really care what others called you, Grace doesn't have to be loud, now does it? By the time your brother and sister came along, he was so thankful we all survived that he didn't care what I named them. Besides, he liked the idea of twin's names that sounded alike. So he and I had a beloved, graceful, strong, victorious family. If I could have given him a name, it would have been, Kavi, a wise man." We both smiled and then she did fall asleep for the rest of the drive.

CHAPTER EIGHT:

When we finally pulled into the house, Honey came rushing down the stairs to help me get Momma out of the car. After we got her upright and moving, Honey wrapped her arm around Momma's waist and slowly walked her up the steps and into the house. I grabbed our bags and set them on the porch, then drove the car into the driveway and left it there. By the time I made it into the house, Momma was sitting in her favorite chair with her feet up, a blanket laid over her lap and a cup of hot sweet tea which was Honey's fix for anything. Remembering the story I had been told, I smiled, "Thanks, Mary."

She looked startled for a second then smiled back, "Oh Sweetie, it's been awhile since someone called me that. Both times I got married the minister asked this Mary lady if she did and I had to think who was Mary. I never really did feel married."

"How did everyone start calling you, Honey?" I asked.

"It started with my Maw, she was a bit on the lazy side, of course having a baby a year every year, sometimes two is hard on a woman," she chuckled "So I can give her a little leeway, now. She knew I was eager to please, so she'd yell, 'Honey, do … this and Honey do … that. And then the other kids started giving me 'Honey do' jobs and it just stuck. When I married your grandfather he asked me if I'd like to go back to Mary, but I said, 'No Sir, I'm Honey, now, I'd just prefer that.'"

"Did you always call your husband Sir?"

"Well every now and then I'd call him Mr. Teague."

"For the entire time you were married you called him Mr. Teague or Sir?" I was incredulous, were they into some form of dominance/submission thing way back then?

She laughed, "I sure did. I called my second husband by his name, Leonard, but my first was more like my father. He was always formal with me too. You know, he never broke a promise he made in his life. I respected that and I respected him."

"Respected, not loved?"

"Respect and like, but no not that kind of love. That kind of love – the sticking, say whatever you want to say in the heat of an argument, accept the person for who he is without reservation, Biblical kind of patient, kind, and keeping them in line love? That comes along only once in a person's life. I found it with Leonard and your momma had it with her Callaway." I must have looked sad because she added, "It's easy to see that you and Steve are struggling, sometimes, you love someone but when you feel their pain it's too much for a human to bear combined with their own. You and Steve have been through too much, it's harder on a marriage than anyone knows. You get to where you quit sharing, and just start feeling, then you quit feeling because you quit sharing. That's what tears a marriage apart, when the feelings stop. If you are angry or hurt, that's probably a good sign. If you are not, then there's no fixing it." With those words of wisdom, she went back into the kitchen to fix us some lunch.

For a few minutes I stood there just staring out the window into the afternoon. The sun shone brightly and the plants and grass stood still, without even a breath of a breeze to move them. A dust cloud billowed from the far field, the farmer Momma rented out the land to must be setting out his tomato plants and tending the fields. It took a great deal of time and effort to truly take care of the land. In order to be successful, a farmer paid attention to everything that affected the earth, from the weather patterns to the type of soil. It took care to understand that when certain crops grew in the field for too long, it destroyed the land; a good farmer knew which crops helped the land, and which crops took from it. He rotated those crops in order to keep his land, as well as himself nourished. And, sometimes, no matter how much attention he

130

paid, no matter how much he cared, the land or the weather would turn on him. Tornadoes, rot, drought, wild animals, floods, even the tiniest worms and mites could destroy an entire crop in seconds or in stages.

A farmer stayed resilient, he kept on year after year after year, hoping and praying and loving and paying attention to his land until, eventually, his family planted him in it. I liked to think that farmers were, for the most part, happy. We lived like that growing up, we raised our own crops of corn, tomatoes, potatoes, and many other fruits and vegetables; raised bees for honey; cows, pigs, chickens and turkey for meat, eggs and fertilizer; mined coal for warmth; hunted for extra meat and mushrooms and ginseng to sell; picked fruits in the orchards and persimmons that grew wild. We learned to care for and love the land, and it cared for us in return.

As I stared outside, I noticed a man walking towards the house carrying a gallon bucket in each hand. His stride looked so familiar, I recognized him before I even saw his face. He walked up to the porch and grinned, "Well, hello, Vani! I didn't know you would be here!"

Kevin. My first love, the one who my pseudo husband resembled stood in front of me. I drank in the details of him first. Time had been kind to him. A few silver strands wove through his dark brown hair. Smile lines bracketed his eyes and mouth. His body had thickened, but retained a muscular firmness. He dressed like a farmer, a very light long sleeve white shirt tucked into blue jeans and dusty work boots.

He handed me the buckets, "The early peaches are on and I thought maybe your mom would feel better with some to eat." He sat the buckets down on the porch, and suddenly, I found myself in his arms with my head on his chest, his arms wrapped around me. For the first time in years, I felt true peace. His hand came up and stroked the back of my head and we hugged tight and rocked back and forth on the porch. He gave the best hugs, put his entire being into them, I forgot how strong and firm he would hold me. Finally, I stepped back.

"Oh my god," I managed to choke out, "What are you doing here?"

"I'm leasing the farm again this year," he replied. At my puzzled look he explained, "I've leased it since the year after your dad died."

"I didn't know that!" I exclaimed!

"I wonder why they didn't tell you."

It didn't matter, I drew back and looked up at him. I wanted to etch him right into my brain. "Do you have time to sit and catch up?"

"I have a few minutes, then I have to get home," he replied.

"Wait here for a second," I took the peaches into the kitchen, poured two glasses of sweat tea, checked on Momma fast asleep in her bed and stepped back out onto the porch. Kevin sat on the top step, I handed him his tea and he drank most of it in one big swallow.

"Thanks, that is really good, it's hot out here," he said.

"You're welcome." Suddenly, I felt shy with him. I know I just hugged him, but the fact remained, the last time I saw him (other than as my pseudo husband) was over twenty-five years ago. The silence stretched out just a little too long to be comfortable, "So," I broke it, nervously, "tell me what you have been up to."

He smiled at me with that smile that always made my heart beat faster. Then he stood up and asked, "Can I have another glass of tea? I think this talk may make me thirsty."

I laughed and went to get another one for him. I also added some cookies Honey had just baked that morning on a plate. I ran to the bathroom, but just sighed when I looked in the mirror. My hair was pulled back into a messy ponytail, I had on jeans and a plain pink tee shirt and no make-up. I stayed in the hospital with Momma every day for the last week and my skin looked pale with dark circles beneath my eyes. I sure didn't look my best, I reminded myself

Kevin came to bring Momma peaches, not to see me. I went back to the kitchen to pick up the glass and plate and headed to the door. As I stepped out onto the porch, he was slowly swinging on the porch swing, I walked to him and settled in beside him, where we used to sit. For several long minutes, we just sat there, watching the fading light, feeling each other's body heat as we swung back and forth. If this had been when we were dating, he would have laid his arm across my shoulders and rubbed absent circles on my arm. I would have rubbed his leg, as far up as I dared with my parents and brother and sister there around us. He would lean over and kiss me and I…

"Where did you go, Lavani?" his deep voice tickled my ear.

"Somewhere far in the past," I laughed.

"I've missed these simple times. I know it's been twenty-five years, but I really want to talk to you."

"I'm listening," I replied.

"When we started dating, you were all I could think about. You were so pretty, still are, and all the boys wanted you. I couldn't believe when I was the lucky one you chose." I listened intently, enjoying that he was close to me, he was the only one who ever made me feel pretty. "I loved you with all my heart. I almost wish we hadn't met until we were a lot older. It seemed like I could just look at you and read your mind we were so close. I couldn't believe it when you gave me your virginity. I swore to myself that you were it, the one, the only one I would ever love. My one true love. We went so far, so fast. Suddenly, I started having so many doubts. I was only 18, you were 16 and you were there, talking marriage and kids and grandkids. Hell, you knew how many kids we'd have and what their names were. You had our whole future mapped out in your head. It's not your fault, but you were just so damn sure of everything. I wasn't. The boys teased me about being whipped, my parents pushed me to get out of town, and honestly, I just was not ready. But, I wanted to be. I tried to be."

"But, I never meant to push you. You never said this to me so that I could stop." I interrupted.

"Part of me didn't want you to stop. I wanted that pretty picture you painted for me. Then I met Callie."

"The woman in the pool hall?" I asked, frowning.

"Yes. She was only a year older than me, though she did look older. She was hot for me. It was exciting sneaking around and having sex and drinking and smoking. She even brought me a joint once. God, I was in so much trouble when I got home and Pops found me eating the leftovers from supper, red eyed and smelling of pot." He chuckled, "I never did that again."

There was a long pause, I waited for him to continue. "I didn't know how to tell you. So, I let you set me up."

"You knew? You knew I was coming there and broke my heart??" I questioned incredulously.

"Yes, I knew. Patti could never keep a secret and she told my best friend your plans."

By this time I was sitting up straight. "Kevin Lee Foster! You broke my heart." Ridiculously, my eyes had tears in them after all these years. "You should have just told me!"

"I couldn't tell you. I couldn't watch you suffer pain because of me. By the time I came to my senses, and was ready to come crawling back, you were getting ready to go to college and had started dating that Phelps boy. Then, Callie told me she was pregnant, with twins." he declared.

"That's the oldest trick in the book," I said in disgust.

"Well, I know that now. I didn't then. We became engaged, my parents were thinking you weren't such a bad choice then," he chuckled. I leaned back again, it just felt so good to feel his body next to mine, that solid, warm flesh I had adored as a teenager. "When it became apparent she was never pregnant, we broke up. I went looking for you. Remember, we didn't have cell phones back then. I asked Jay where you were, but he punched me in the face."

"Jay punched you?" I was shocked, godly perfect Jay had punched someone?"

"Yep. Told me I had it coming for a long time,

but his parents wouldn't let him. He wanted to punch me after word got out that we were parking nights down by the creek. His dad gave him the green light when we broke up."

I sat there, stunned, my DAD wanted to punch him?

"Anyway, I asked him where you were and he didn't tell me. I asked Jayce where you were and she simply froze me out."

I laughed, Jayce's freeze out was legendary. Someone would say something to her and she would look him straight in the eyes, tilt her head, frown, look all the way down and the up his body and turn away without saying a word.

"I couldn't find you anywhere and word got back to me that you hated me and were dating others pretty seriously. I went out to the barn with Aaron (his best friend) and got really drunk and swore I'd never bother you again, but I didn't mean it. So, I went away to college to get my degree. I heard you were getting married the day of the wedding and tried to get there; Aaron stopped me and we just ended up driving around for hours while

I drank and cried. It was too late, but I knew I had let my soul mate go. I went back to college a changed man. I met my ex-wife and we settled down. I had two kids, the family dog, a ranch style house, a car, a truck and a good job. And, I was quietly miserable. We weren't a good fit. It wasn't her fault, she loved me in her way, I think. But, I could only think about you. All these years and you were on my mind. It's not her fault, I'm not blaming her, I take full responsibility for my choices, but I started cheating on her. It was the only excitement in my life. Then, I realized, I was doing to her what I did to you. I wanted her to catch me and divorce me because I wasn't man enough to break her heart. So, I manned up. I went to her and told her that I didn't love her, that I wanted out. Ironically, her response was, 'oh I'm so glad you said it first,' she had found another man. Believe it or not, at first that made me jealous! Now, I wanted her," again, he chuckled. "To make a long story shorter, she stuck to her guns, we divorced, split everything down the middle – including my girls which makes me sad. Now, I only see them every other weekend and holidays and summers. Tonight, they both had dates, which is why I'm here. Now that they are older, I see them less and less."

His story wound down, we sat there in silence. I thought about all he had said, and a weight I hadn't even known lay on my shoulders lifted. He really had loved me back. I never realized what a hit my self-esteem had taken when I saw him kissing and ducking into the back room with that two-bit whore, wow, I guess there was still some anger there. I leaned my head back against his shoulder. His smell drifted over me and we just continued to swing. A long time later, I found my voice. "When I saw you and her, it devastated me. My heart wasn't just broken, it was shattered. I came home and cried all night. I think I cried for several days at a time. I couldn't eat, I couldn't sleep, I couldn't think. I had to study for my finals, and I couldn't concentrate. Then, one night I just decided I was finished with it. I could not cry for the rest of my life. I buckled down, studied hard. Received some scholarships and went away to take courses over that summer, I just couldn't bear to be here. I didn't come home much, I played softball for the college team the first two years and we traveled. And I worked, so my weekends were spent working, playing ball and studying. I graduated in four years even though I got married during my junior year. I met Steve my sophomore year. At first, he reminded me of you. He was tall, thin, and loved sports. I never saw that he loved himself most of all. It was there, I chose not to see it." I thought back to the instances I should have known, when he wouldn't walk me back to the dorm after our dates, when he treated me like I was just a little bit stupid when I asked a question, when he didn't respect my own activities. "Once when I was in a big conference game, I was up to the plate. There were two outs and two people on. The first base coach pointed to the right field line, it was completely open."

He chimed in, "Oh you loved placing the ball. You practiced that a lot."

"Yes, so I hit the ball right on that line, way out in right field. It was the best hit I ever made at the best time. I hit a triple and we won the game. I was so excited! He didn't have a game that day, so he had been there to see me hit it. I just knew how proud he would be of me."

After the team meeting, he was waiting for me. I ran over, "What did you think of my hit?"

"I heard it was a good one."

"Heard? You were right there watching."

"Well, no. I was in the next field over passing ball with the guys. You know softball leagues will be starting soon!"

"But, that was an important game, the only one you've been able to make all year."

"Quit being so damned selfish, I have other things to do besides be with you, you know." And he grabbed my bat bag and flung it way out in the middle of the field. I was humiliated. I ran to get it and just ran back to my dorm room while he stomped away. We argued, but I always forgave, I always do. To do like you and make a long story shorter, that was the week I found out I was pregnant. I told him, so he asked me to marry him, and I agreed. Our entire married life has been about him, what he wants, when he wants, how he wants. I'm not sure I can live that way any longer."

I had never said it out loud to another person before. I couldn't live with someone who didn't value or respect me. It was simply that. I couldn't believe that I opened up so quickly to Kevin. We always possessed a relationship where we could tell each other anything, so it seemed natural to tell him all of this.

After our mutual confessions, we chit chatted for a while, then he stood up. "If you ever decide you want to be single again, give me a call. I'd love to take you out." I watched him walk confidently out to his truck, and admired his little round butt, like I used to do, until he turned around and winked at me. Caught, I smiled at him, we might never see each other again, but finally I had the entire story. It is freeing to know the whys of a situation.

CHAPTER NINE:

Momma was NOT an easy patient. I think it came from years of being the person in charge of the sick room. She became impatient with herself and limited by pain, she hated taking the pain pills that made her sleepy and a little out of her head. We teased her about some of the things she said in her drug induced chats, "Tell that man not to mow over my tomatoes," she shouted out around midnight one night, "I need those tomatoes, how else am I going to feed you children this winter?" I assured her, through my laughter, no man mowed her tomatoes at midnight; but, she muttered about it all the rest of that long night. The most pitiful times, she asked for her Callaway. I finally took a quilt and wrapped it in covers, put a heating pad on it and left it in bed beside her. She was much happier.

We tried to talk to her about making a decision about her treatments. Doctor Rose (the twelve year old asshole twerp had moved on to his next rotation) recommended radiation followed by chemotherapy. If that didn't work to stop the cancer, she recommended just using chemo for palliative purposes. Even if Momma did all the treatments, the doctor couldn't give her more than a year – three months if she did nothing. The cancer had metastasized into her lungs and possibly her brain. It progressed faster than usual, so Momma didn't have much time to decide before it decided for her. If Momma decided to forgo treatment, Dr. Rose recommended that we contact Hospice and set up care for her last few weeks.

On a particularly good night, Momma, Honey and I sat in the living room watching Jeopardy and keeping count of the points. The match volleyed back and forth until the final question dealt with math. Trust me, I lost that one! After the show finished, we switched the television to Antiques Roadshow. I picked up the latest book I was reading and Honey crocheted an afghan to send to one of her grandchildren. Momma looked up and said, "I miss weaving."

"You weave?" I asked, surprised.

She looked surprised that I didn't know, "Well, yes, I used to be very well known for my weaving skills. When I midwifed, it was my custom to give each baby a blanket, I had woven."

"Momma, did you weave Jay's and Jayce's blankets? The blue and green one and the pink and yellow?"

She smiled, "those were the last ones I ever wove. After the twins were born, I didn't midwife anymore. I was just too busy."

"Do I have a blanket?" I hoped the answer was yes.

A very long pause occurred as Momma looked at Honey and Honey nodded back at her slightly in seeming encouragement, "Yes, actually you have two. Both are in the attic."

"Why didn't you give them to me?" I asked, confused.

"It's a long story and I don't want to get into it. I'm tired, I'm going to my room." She stood up, took her book and glasses from the end table and went into her room. I looked at Honey who studiously counted her crochet stitches, obviously not open to explanation.

Feeling ridiculously hurt, I mean come on I'm almost 45, I went into the bathroom to take a long bath while reading my book. After my soak, I went to my bedroom and called Emily and Steve, just to check in on them. I caught Emily as she was getting ready to go out with a bunch of friends. She sounded happy and rushed, and a little relieved when I offered to hang up. Steve was a little more stilted than usual. He didn't want to talk, but the Indians were playing in the background, and I knew how that went. When I heard Honey and Momma getting ready for bed, I went out and helped them with the usual nighttime meds and routine. When I helped lift Momma into the tall bed she and Daddy shared their entire married life, I smoothed the covers and helped her turn to hug the quilt in the middle then kissed her cheek, it struck me how we had almost switched roles. "Lavani, there is a trunk in the attic. Maybe tomorrow you could bring it down. It would be a good place to start talking about some of the things I want to tell you. Both of the blankets are in that."

"OK, Momma, if you feel like it, I will bring it down." I replied sofly.

"There's a lot you need to know, I'm just so tired I can't tell you right now." she said soft but stern.

"It's ok, Momma, I love you." I reassured her.

"I know. I love you, too. I always have." she said quietly.

"Good night, Momma."

"Good night, Lavani," she whispered as she drifted off into sleep.

It was days later, before I went to the attic to get the big box. During the night, I heard her moaning and talking out of her head, she refused her pain meds, other than Advil before bed, so this was not normal. I ran into her room to find her shivering hard under all of the blankets and the heating pad, shaking so hard the entire bed moved with her. We ended up calling the ambulance because her temperature rose to 104 degrees. We got her back to UK and on IV medicines to take care of this infection. After a few days of touch and go, she pulled through. But, all of us could see the toll it took on her. She was much too thin, frail and slow speaking. The cancer growing in her brain robbed her of her essence very quickly. Momma refused to do any kind of treatment, so we knew this extremely limited our time together.

She asked me one day to promise her two things: 1) we wouldn't keep her living on any machines and 2) we would let her die at home. After that talk, I called her doctor and we started Momma with Hospice care. All of us knew her life was entering its final weeks, maybe days, and we wanted her to be comfortable and happy.

Her brain tumor began to cause her to experience some strange symptoms. One of the most amazing ones affected her vision. Instead of seeing what we saw, she experienced beautiful colors and textures. One day as we sat on the porch talking and breaking beans, she exclaimed, "Oh my goodness, look at that light!"

It was rather cloudy outside, so I asked, "Which light, Momma?"

"It's so very bright. The outside edges are sparkling like diamonds and the inside of it is too bright to look at directly. I wonder if that is God and all of his angels." Her breathless wonder continued, "Now it's turning in a circle and it looks like a kaleidoscope: hot pink, dark blue, grass green and Tiffany blue. Oh my, it is so beautiful."

Her face held a reverent look as she described the colors and textures only she saw. I cried. Thankfully, she didn't see my tears. I offered up gratitude to the cosmos that she saw

153

only beauty, nothing frightened her. Sometimes, she thought she saw my daddy and she held long conversations with him. They discussed their children and the farm, he held her hand while she rocked on the porch. It was pitiful, yet quite beautiful in its own way. Their love endured until the bittersweet end.

Kevin came to visit, a shorter one this time. He brought us a bushel of tomatoes and a couple of pecks of green peppers. I gave him some peach jelly I made from the ones he picked. We talked on the porch again, and hugged and he left. He didn't stay long, but I felt a special glow as I walked into the house. This time, Honey stood there looking at me speculatively, "You need to be careful, Lavi. If you play with fire, you're going to get burned," she cautioned.

"We aren't doing anything but talking," I replied defensively.

"It don't look like it's talking that put that glow on your face."

"Whatever, Honey," I rudely walked off. I mean, who did she think she was, Jiminy Cricket? I possessed my own conscience, I didn't need her to add to it. Actually, I already felt quite a bit of guilt. Kevin and I exchanged numbers soon after our first talk on the porch and spent the evenings and nights texting each other. We poured our hearts out to each other, and then started flirting. The night before, I sent him a picture of my cleavage in my gown. I felt guilty, but I also felt alive. I didn't want to stop. I wanted to explore these feelings swirling inside my heart for the first time since I left home as a very young adult.

Steve seldom called me and never texted, when I called him, the conversations drug on, stilted and mostly silent until I fabricated an excuse to hang up. With Kevin, we never ran out of things to talk about. Pseudo husband definitely wore Kevin's face now, and the conversations in my heard sounded remarkably like the ones we texted the night before. I wanted to grow farther in this relationship, but I still held back. Steve and I stuck together through some pretty hard circumstances for twenty-five years. He nursed me when I became sick with cancer and held me when my sorrow for Christian drowned me. I knew that somewhere buried in his heart, he loved me in his own way. I simply could not drive into his relationship with himself.

I also knew, Kevin may appear to be perfect now; but, he was human. He admitted that he cheated on his wife; if I cheated on Steve with Kevin, what would be trustworthy about either of us? How would we be assured that there was no boyfriend or girlfriend in the wings any time we had trouble? We couldn't. I didn't want to be that woman. That woman who cheated on her husband, who wasn't trustworthy. But, I wanted to be the woman who was loved, admired and sought after. I wanted that companionship I saw in my parent's marriage. I ping ponged from side to side in my mind. This unrest caused lots of sleepless nights and restless thoughts.

Several days after returning from the hospital as we ate lunch, Momma appeared especially alert and put her sandwich down on her plate "Lavani, I need you to go upstairs into the attic and bring down a small steamer trunk for me. You will find it in the middle of the room. Be careful."

So, I went up to the attic and drug down a box that would both change and explain, my life.

CHAPTER TEN:

I drug the steamer trunk into the living room, then ran to get a wet cloth to wipe off the dust at Momma's direction. She slowly knelt beside the trunk to lift the lid, I got her a short stool to sit on instead. She lifted the lid to a full trunk. Inside there were many items, there were two woven blankets. One was pink and traditional with little flecks of yellow and green in it. The other was disturbing, most of it was a blood red and had black and stark white spots in random places. Although it was the size of a baby blanket, it certainly was not intended for a baby. It shocked me to look at it, to see the pain and anger in it. Is that what she felt when she was carrying me? I looked at her and she looked steadily back, meeting my gaze with a strength I had not seen in weeks. She was ready to tell me the truth. I laid the blankets aside and dug a little deeper, unearthing a few large scrapbooks, a set of thick journals, and other items that women keep. There was also a tiny delicate white dress and cap, embroidered and detailed with tiny stitches that evoked flowers in the garden, they were of pinks and greens so pale, they looked almost white. It was gorgeous. I picked it up out of the tissue paper, reverently, and a small picture floated out of its folds. A baby, wearing it, in the arms of my mother with my father smiling over her shoulder with pride and love. My mother looked nervous and held the baby awkwardly. She was a beautiful baby with thick black curly hair that nearly reached her shoulders, her eyes were wide open with a somberness most babies do not show, and her cheeks were full.

"Is this Jayce? Where is Jay?" I asked.

Momma smiled, "Lavani, that is you."

I was stunned, if I looked closely, I could see my Emily, at that age. "I never knew I was a pretty baby," I blurted out. Momma looked at me quizzically, "Sweety, you never have been able to see your own beauty. Even now, you can't see it. Honey made you that cap and dress. I've always told her she could make a lot of money doing her embroidery, but she would only do it for new babies and brides."

She stacked the journals in an order that made sense to her, laid the scrapbooks beside them in another order and then sat back, exhausted with her efforts. "I wanted to tell you the whole story, but I don't have the words. I think if you read the journals, you will understand better. Plus, I can answer any questions you might still have. I've also talked to Honey and she can tell you everything. She knows it all. If something happens to me before we finish, she can finish my story." I helped her up and then slowly made our way to her bedroom, gave her the pain medication that helped her rest, and gently lifted her into bed. She had always been thin, but now she was almost emaciated. Damn cancer.

I picked up the journals and stacked them in her order back in the trunk and laid the scrapbooks beside them and carried it into my room to stand beside my bed. I then gathered up the dress and blankets and put them, gently, into drawers to protect them from sunshine and dust. I found that I was putting off reading, like if I didn't read them, I wouldn't have to know. I wanted to know everything, yet I wanted to know nothing. I decided to take a walk instead, but at the last minute picked up the top journal and slipped it into a bag with a bottle of water and my cell phone.

I left a note on the table for Honey, telling her I had my phone in case she needed me and slipped out of the house by the back door then headed straight back to my spot in the woods. This peaceful spot belonged only to me. I found it one day when I roamed the woods looking for adventure at the age of eight. I sat down on a large flat yellow rock that hung over a swiftly moving creek. The trees formed a canopy over my head, shielding me from the worst of the sunlight, but as the leaves moved in the slight breeze, a little would sneak through and dapple the rock and shine on me with bright light. I used to pretend that the sunlight shone on the diamonds I wore all over my body to indicate my royalty. Now, I just enjoyed the warmth and hypnotic play of light and shadow. The rock itself felt always a little warm, even in winter, and in the middle of it lay a depression just the size of my body now. It used to be too big for me, but I grew into it.

I leaned back into that spot and put my arms under my head and gazed upwards at the trees. I could hear the little creek babbling and talking to me, excited with the rain from the night before. I imagined it telling me the secrets of the fairies, if only I could understand its language. I had written poems and descriptions of this spot many times, and essentially it stayed the same from season to season from year to year from decade to decade. I had come here as a child and dangled my feet into the water. I read books here, played with my siblings here, cried here and thought here. After my son, Christian, died I came here one day and screamed. I screamed until I became so hoarse I could not scream more. That day, I recognized the new woman living in my soul. I called her Rachel, after the lady in the Bible from Matthew 2:18:

"A voice is heard in Ramah, weeping and great mourning, Rachel weeping for her children and refusing to be comforted because they are no more." Rachel lived in me now. Always that mother inside me screamed and wailed, grieved and wept. There could be no comfort, because my son was no more. I named her here at this rock, but I have lived with her since my son passed.

Those days will not leave my mind. Christian was so sick. He was on life support, but conscious and able to move around. We would take walks every single day, it was what the doctor wanted, so he, his nurse, his physical therapist, his perfusionist (the person who guarded the life support system) and I would walk. Sometimes we would simply walk around the ICU block, but sometimes he felt really well and we would walk out a back way and sit in the sunshine. He would lift his face to the clouds and close his eyes and just breathe. He said everywhere else, the smell of his oxygen would interfere with the real smells, but here he could smell the outside. The last day we went out, he collapsed on the way back and we had to push him back to the room in a chair. Two days later he struggled so hard to breathe he requested to be trached and ventilated. Two days after that, he lost consciousness and two days after that, he died.

We let his physical body go on a Saturday afternoon. But, that which made him Christian left sooner. Wednesday, he had been restless, the bells we put around his wrist rang all day as he motioned he needed to be rolled over, moved or pillows tucked. He kept mouthing the word, "sing" to me. I'm a terrible singer, but in his last days he kept asking me to sing to him the songs, I sang to him as a child. So, I sang. I sat between the life support machine, the dialysis machine and his IV pole and held his hand and I sang, "You Are My Sunshine," I sang, "I Love You, Christian," I sang a little song I made up for him about what we would do when he received his lungs and felt strong and good. It was about driving his car, playing golf, playing baseball and doing all the things he loved to do. He smiled every time I sang it. When I had to get up

165

to let a nurse in, or use the restroom, he would purse his lips to me for a kiss, and I would kiss that great big boy right on his 17 year old lips. And I would kiss his head and I would tell him I loved him and I was so proud of him. I would whisper, be strong, our miracle is coming. I even promised him that, and I had never broken a promise to him. I promised him he would be OK.

That whole day, from around two in the morning until almost four the next morning, I sat and held his hand and sang. Finally, my husband convinced me to go home and sleep. My son was finally resting, his dad was by his side, one of his favorite nurses was in charge, so I went and I slept.

I awoke at about eight o'clock that morning, stunned by a feeling of loss so intense I couldn't breathe. I knew I needed to get ready and go back right away, so I got in the shower. I sobbed the entire time. I prayed the entire time. I dressed, still crying and went into the bedroom and dropped by the bed to my knees and I prayed and I begged and I cried. But, the loss still crushed me. As I drove into UK Parking Garage, I recognized it, it was the connection a mother has with her child. That invisible chain from heart to heart that tunes her in so that she knows her child is OK. It is the chain the child tugs as he grows, but also as he needs her. My chain was disconnected. My son was no longer on the other end. I ran from the parking garage to the hospital room. I ran into the room. My husband sat beside the bed holding his hand, he had not let go; but, the nurse was beside the other side with tears in his eyes. He looked up and quietly told me to come look. He moved his flashlight into my son's eyes and they did not react. They were fixed and dilated – a term that I came to understand meant that which was my son was gone. He had left while I was not there to hold his hand on the way out.

Since then, I have been told that sometimes souls cannot let go of the physical body if someone they love is in the room and grieving. I think he waited until I was gone because he knew how much I loved him.

I did not let go of his hand that day. We went to scans and xrays and different tests, doctors came in and out of the room, whispering with serious eyes and quiet voices. I would not let go of him. I think I thought if I let go again, he would be gone for sure. The next morning his doctor came in, in tears, the brain scans showed that Christian was gone. He was brain dead. He had been since the morning before. It was time to let him go. We had already called all the family in to wish him good-bye, but we came to find out he had already said good-bye to each person in his own way. They waited for us in the waiting room of the ICU, along with the nurses from the Children's Hospital, the Doctors who cared for him, the friends who could make it, and all the strangers who had become friends in our long stay there. They held vigil for him.

Steve, Emily and I stayed with him until the last moment. I climbed up into his bed, wrapped my arms around his shoulders, my head next to his and told him how much I loved him and how proud and blessed I was to be his momma until the last machine was turned off and his body quit functioning. But, I couldn't sing. I couldn't do that for him. I whispered the words of "You Are My Sunshine," to him, but I failed him in the end. I could not comfort him with his songs. Already, inside, Rachel was screaming. I begged and I prayed and I bargained and I truly believed there would be a miracle. There wasn't one. That day, I left both my son's body and my God's body in that room to prepare for burial. I left my heart and I left my soul.

I went to this rock, because I knew once I opened those journals my life would change, and more, because I was ready for my life to change. I knew I was tired of living the routine, doing what was easiest for me because I didn't want to rock the boat. I knew that I was finished with doing things for appearances' sake and that it was time to begin to control my life, instead of letting it control me. I laid on that rock, and I imagined the strength and solidity of it rising through the earth and into my body. "I am a rock," I said. Then laughed because I thought of

Simon and Garfunkel. "I am rock solid, I am steadfast I am grounded deep and cannot be moved."

PART 2:

Sarah's Story

CHAPTER ELEVEN:

Sarah

She liked to pretend that she could move silently, like her mother's people, the townspeople called them Cherokee, but her mother called her people Yun'Wiya. She slipped from tree trunk to tree trunk, avoiding loose rocks and twigs on the ground that could give her presence away, though her quarry was loud and would probably not hear her anyway. She moved swiftly, like those she followed, silently so no alarm could be sounded as she watched and learned their life patterns and habits. Daily, almost, she awaited their arrival to the woods, some days they did not come, some days they were loud and reckless, one of them came once and cried. Today, she had decided, she would make contact. As she raced through the woods, then the public streets, following them, she wondered what their reactions would be, these look alike boys. Would they turn their heads away and ignore her, as adults often did, or throw rock and say hateful words, like "half-breed," and "redskin," as the children did. She followed them to a giant mountain of dirt and watched in fascination as they wrestled at the top, almost violently, yelling and whooping and saying hateful words with obvious love. Harder and harder they wrestled, oblivious to her as she slipped up behind them. Ahhh, they were playing a game, "King of the Mountain," hmmmm… she silently stepped behind them, put her hands in the small of their backs and shoved, hard, she was stronger than she looked, then watched as they both tumbled down the mountain. Before she could think it through, she shouted, "I am QUEEN of the mountain!" Then, seeing the shock and disbelief on those faces, the same brown eyes looking up at her in amazement, she froze in terror. She couldn't move as predator became prey and they surged up the mountain towards her.

Two sets of identical eyes looked at her, but their expressions were different. One had a grudging respect, though a pride and anger deep inside that scared her. The other, held respect and humor, and something no one had ever looked at her with, she didn't know the name of it, but it warmed her, made her lean toward him, more. "Wow!!" he shouted, "How did you do that??"

The other brother scowled, "It was luck, she took us by surprise, is all." He elbowed the one with the kind eyes, "Betcha she couldn't do it again!"

The other one was looking at her steadily and with great wisdom in his eyes, "I'm going to marry you someday, so I better know your name."

"Ah, it's Sarah," she almost whispered, straightening in anger when the other one said, "Come on Callaway, it's that oldest half-breed of old man Teague's, we go to school with her."

"Sarah is a pretty name, and you are a pretty girl," said the one called Callaway. He glared at his brother, "Colton, don't you talk

175

about my future wife that way!" He raised his fist as he said it.

"Forget it," his brother muttered, "I didn't mean anythin' by it, I don't care what she is. Come on, we're gonna be late for dinner and Mom will skin us!"

"Wait," she blurted, "Can I play with you guys sometime? Tomorrow?"

"Sure," Callaway said with a smile, "we play ball on the playground every day, I've seen you watching, bring your mitt, we'll put you on our team." With that glorious promise, they raced back down the mountain and into the woods.

Sarah watched them go with a lightness in her heart she'd never known. They didn't care if she was a half breed she planned to marry one and play with the other. No one played with her, ever, or her brothers and sisters, but these rough and wild boys would tomorrow. She hugged her arms around herself and tasted tears on her mouth, though she couldn't figure out when she cried.

The next day, Sarah brought the mitt that the Old Methodist Mission had put into a box of give away clothes. She waited patiently, silently, as the teams were picked. Of course, Colton and Callaway were each captains. Finally, when there were only three kids standing there, Callaway winked at her, "I'll take Sarah," he said.

One of the boys he had chosen in the first couple of rounds protested, "Oh come on, Man, why do we have to have the dirty Redskin?"

Sarah felt her face flush and she looked down at her shoes wishing she could just sink right into the ground. She was so embarrassed, now Callaway would realize she was half Indian and he wouldn't want her on his team. Maybe he wouldn't want to marry her anymore, either. Well, fine then, she straightened her shoulders and lifted her chin and stared right into Callaway's steady gaze, he nodded at her, "I want Sarah, if you don't want to be on my team, you can join Colton's," he calmly said to the rude boy. And they took the field.

After that day, school wasn't as hard for Sarah. She learned to expect that when she raised her hand to answer a question, the teacher called on her only when she alone knew the answer. She learned that the other little girls weren't allowed to play with her, or sit with her at lunch time. She learned that she was smarter than most of them, and that the teacher would still give her the A's she deserved, even if she wouldn't call on her or brag on her like she did the other kids. But all day, from the time she woke up in the morning she looked forward to recess because she knew that no matter what game they were playing, or how bad at it she was, Callaway would pick her. He would pick her for his team regardless of the teasing and name calling. She tugged her brothers along with her and he picked them, too. But, at least they played well. Sarah tried to get her sister to play, but she refused. He even turned the joke back onto the boys and girls who would ridicule her brothers and her and call the teams the Chiefs, the Indians, the Redskins, whatever term they used that day, and they won almost every game. He simply would not allow his team to lose. By then, they had at least become tolerated, if not accepted, and Sarah had developed a massive case of hero worship for the handsome young man who, still insisted he would be her husband one day when they grew up.

Every day after school, Sarah and her brothers and sisters walked the long road home. Once there, they changed into their work clothes and neatly hung their school clothes in the closet, then they headed out to do their chores. The boys would go to the barn and muck out the horse stall, feed and water the horse, then milk both of the cows. They would bring the milk into the house for Mother. Sarah, would then return to the barn, or field or pasture, or tobacco stripping room, wherever Father had them working that day. Sarah and the girls would help Mother in the house. Usually when they got home from school, the house would be clean. If it was a weekend, they would wake up and make up the beds, sweep the floors, dust the furniture, and help with cooking and dishes. During the week, they helped with the vegetable garden, helped

179

preserve the food, cook dinner and serve and do the dishes afterward. After the dishes were done, the children would sit around the big dinner table and work on their homework, taking turns reading aloud from their lessons and helping each other as needed. Sarah loved these times, she loved learning how to put sounds to letters and letters into words and words into sentences. She loved learning how to spell, the teacher couldn't ignore her during a spelling bee when it was her turn, so she spent extra time practicing her spelling so that every Friday afternoon, she could beat every kid in her class.

Lavani

I smiled as I read this. Momma's competitiveness was legendary in our home. She never let anyone win anything, no matter what age her competitor. We played some intense rounds of Scrabble and beating her felt like winning a gold medal at the Olympics. Once, I walked into the kitchen after a Sunday lunch and found her and Emily giving each other the hairy eyeball over a game of Chutes and Ladders. I laughed and left the room. When Emily skipped in, I asked, "Who won?"

"Grammy did, she always wins. Then she gave me a piece of cake," she smiled at me and ran out. I teased Momma who giggled and helped us pack up to leave.

Sarah

One evening as Sarah studied, she looked up and around the room. She, her oldest sister and her three brothers sat at the table, all of their heads bent over a book, or a sheet of paper doing math problems. Father rocked in his chair, smoking his pipe, reading the newspaper with his glasses on and slowly rocking. Mother rested beside him in a slightly smaller chair sewing a patch on a pair of her brother's pants, they always got holes in the knees. One of the younger sisters slept on the floor, thumb in mouth and one lay in front of the couch playing with her paper dolls. The radio played the news in the background. As she looked closer at her mother, she saw her belly was swollen with the addition of another child. Sarah felt the beauty of her family for the very first time, the acceptance they each had of the other and the peace of the evening crept into her spirit. She prayed to the God her father had taught her about, and then Unetlanvhi her mother had secretly taught her about, in thanks for this family. She thought about the story her mother told her on Saturday.

Sarah had been complaining because Father had taken the boys fishing, she knew they would get to skinny dip in the creek and it was hot in the house where she and her sisters and mother were working. She was churning butter

182

and said, "I wish I had been born a boy. Maybe Father would want to talk to me."

Her mother quietly smiled, "Most animals hope for girls you know. My mother used to tell me the story about the wren and cricket," and she began in the sing song voice she used to tell stories.

"The little Wren is the messenger of the birds, and pries into everything. She gets up early in the morning and goes round to every house in the settlement to get news for the bird council. When a new baby is born she finds out whether it is a boy or girl and reports to the council, If it is a boy the birds sing in mournful chorus: "Alas! the whistle of the arrow! my shins will burn," because the birds know that when the boy grows older he will hunt them with his blowgun and arrows and roast them on a stick.

But if the baby is a girl, they are glad and sing: "Thanks! the sound of the pestle! At her home I shall surely be able to scratch where she sweeps," because they know that after a while they will be able to pick up stray grains where she beats the corn into meal. When the Cricket hears that a girl is born, it also is glad, and says, "Thanks, I shall sing in the house where she lives. "But if it is a boy the Cricket laments: "Alas! He will shoot me! He will shoot me! He will shoot me!" because boys make little bows to shoot crickets and grasshoppers. "

She loved it when Mother told her native stories. She only did when Father wasn't around because, he wanted the children to be raised as Christians. They dressed in their best clothes and went to church every time the doors were open. He had insisted that Mother be baptized into his faith, though Sarah thought he knew but would never admit, she never really believed in his God. But, when the family was there, the congregation would not sit close to them, nor would they shake their hands during the time of welcome. They would enter the building in silence (children were never allowed to speak in church) go to their pew on the left side near the front and sit completely still on the hard seats she had heard called pews. The congregation would

184

sing a song then a man would stand and lead a long prayer about sin and Jesus, they would pray again then the harsh looking pastor always dressed in black would stand behind the pulpit and start talking. He'd talk for a while, but then he would start shouting and jumping up and down and saying things she couldn't understand and his behavior would frighten her, because she knew that soon the congregation would join in. They would moan at first, then start shouting "amen," then they would stand with their arms up in the air and some would dance. The preacher would keep shouting and sometimes other people would lay on the floor and shake or lay as stiff as a board, while others would shout around them.   Sarah would sit in her seat, shaking and wishing she could escape. But, they would stay until the preacher quit shouting, the people were in their seats again and crying and another long prayer. Sometimes, they were there for hours and her bottom and back would ache when she stood up and she'd have to try not to stomp to wake up her feet.   They would walk quietly out of the door where the preacher would shake Father's hand and pretend not to see her mother or their children.

The times she hated the most, however, were the times when the preacher would call someone to the front at the altar. He would make that person stand there while he told the congregation what he or she had done wrong, or what he thought they had done wrong. They would stand there while he preached about their particular sin and have to repent publicly. Most would cry and beg him for his forgiveness. Their families would be embarrassed, but would surround them when they were allowed to go back to their seats. But, there was one young woman she remembered most.

The preacher called her to the front, and told her to bring her new baby with her. Her husband walked up the aisle behind her and stood beside her with his arm on her shoulder as she protectively held the baby close. The preacher announced to the congregation that their baby was sick, and she stayed sick because her mother did not have the faith to allow her to heal. He prayed for her and quoted a line about faith and mustard seeds. This woman did not cry, nor did her husband. Instead, they stood there and listened for a while with no expressions and stiff backs. This seemed to make the preacher angry and he shouted louder until he was right in their faces. Suddenly, the man squeezed his wife's shoulder, she looked up and him and he nodded slightly, then quietly led her down the aisle. She met my mother's eyes as she left, there were tears of pity in them, then reached down and touched her hand, then continued to walk on. They walked right out the door of the church with the preacher following them and yelling at them about Hell and Damnation. When he shut the door, he announced they were now dead to everyone in the church. If anyone wanted to associate with them, they could no longer come back to the church until they repented. In shock, they watched as the girl's parents, a Deacon and his hard working wife, rose from their pew and also left the church. The boy's parents stayed, with lips tightly folded. The couple and her parents never came back to the church, Sarah heard they had switched congregations. The preacher often used them as examples of hard headed-ness and closed hearts, but Sarah knew they were active in the community and always seemed to be where people needed help. Plus, that was the only person in the church who had ever touched her mother. She hoped, if the day came, she could stand there with her head held high.

She would never tell her father, but she much preferred her mother's religion. Once she had asked her mother, "Why did you get baptized?"

Her mother just looked peaceful and said, "A dunk under the water is a small way to keep peace in the house. It's never a bad thing to get a bath. You know, Sarah, it is not a bad faith if you listen to the Messiah. Jesus tried to teach them to love and accept everyone. They just don't listen to him. I'd like Jesus if I met him, I bet he lived like the Yun'Wiya. One of my favorite parts of the Bible your daddy reads us is when the children want to be with Jesus and he lets them.

Children don't want to be around people who are mean or grumpy, they like those who laugh and play. That tells me Jesus played with them."

They smiled at each other, then her mother told her another story about the rabbit and they continued on with their day.

Once she told her mother how much she loved her name, Charlotte. She laughed and responded, "Only the white people call me that, my real name is Chandrika. It means 'Moonlight'. I was born on the night of a full moon and my father said it was so beautiful, he wanted his daughter to always remember."

Sarah, puzzled, asked, "Then why doesn't Father call you by your real name?"

Mother smiled at her, "He wanted me to give up my ways for him. He can't see past the color of my skin and keeps trying to change it, even though he loves me." She sighed, "I think he wishes he didn't, I am an embarrassment to him."

Sarah looked at her mother, she was a small woman, short and slight. Her belly was full with child and her face was serene, as always. She moved in grace and with a fluidity Sarah often tried to copy. "Mother, you are beautiful, not an embarrassment."

That was one of their last conversations. Soon after that her mother went into premature labor. She labored for two days until, finally, her father sent for the doctor. The doctor refused to come sending a message that he was not a veterinarian and would not help an animal give birth. If she needed help, she should call her own people. Sarah's little brother had punched him in the stomach for that and received a hard slap and shove in return. She wished she had had the chance to punch that Doctor too. Her mother, in pain and feverishness, requested her shaman from her tribe, but Father said no, he wasn't going to allow heathens to take care of her. Her beautiful mother died in that hot and airless room, along with her baby, with no one to help relieve her pain.

Sarah hated the doctor after that, and refused to repent. When she saw him in church, she would stare at him with flat expressionless eyes that unnerved him. She pretended she was a warrior, staking out her enemy. When he looked at her, she would not look away, she just allowed her contempt for him to show, when he walked by her, she would spit in the roadway behind him. He must have complained to her father, but she was never punished for it.

At school, soon after the funeral of her mother, Callaway sat beside her where she sat listlessly watching the other kids play. "Sarah, I just want you to know, me and Colton, we're going to make him regret not takin' care of your momma. We're goin' to get him good."

Later that week, she heard that the doctor's house had been egged, his trees wrapped in paper, nasty words spray painted on his barn and sugar put into his gas tank. No one ever found out who did it, but the day before, Callaway had grinned and winked at her. She never told. No one ever told, though many must have known. Even though her mother had never been accepted, the community still saw her as one of "their own". The doctor didn't care for "their own" and people began to stop going to him. Soon after, the doctor moved away, no one came to take his place, if someone got sick, they had to go a couple of towns over for a doctor. But, a nurse-midwife named Natalie moved into his house, painted the barn a bright red and took care of anyone and everyone who came to her door.

Natalie quickly took to Sarah and her family. She loved spending time with them and tended to their cuts and bruises as tenderly as an aunt. She, in fact told them they reminded her, in many ways, of her sister's family. Sarah spent hours there at her house, going through her medical books, the ones about labor and birth fascinated her. Natalie laughed and said most people were a little bit disgusted by the pictures, but Sarah drank in the knowledge. She never wanted anyone else to lose a mother, wife, friend or family member because of not knowing what to do. She determined she would become a nurse-midwife herself. Later, she assisted Natalie whenever she could and learned first-hand what it meant to be a nurse-midwife, both the heart-ache and the joy.

Sarah once told Natalie her biggest fear. She had not insisted that her father put her mother's Yun'Wiya name on her headstone; she feared her mother's gods might not recognize her. Natalie assured her that they would find her, that the soul's name was spoken in the wind, not on a tombstone.

Truth and Grace

CHAPTER TWELVE:

Lavani

I looked up and noticed the twilight falling and realized I lost track of time while reading Momma's first journal. I thought about the kind of racism she faced growing up in the 40's and 50's. People tended to focus on Martin Luther King, Jr and the racism associated with African Americans, but racism loomed everywhere, even directed to a small child and her Cherokee Mother, no wonder my momma become a nurse-midwife, that lady had to have been the first person she saw who didn't judge people on the color of their skin.

With a sigh, I pushed myself up off the rock, I was stiff from sitting on it for so long and knew I needed to return to the house to help. I couldn't wait to get back into her journals. When I checked my phone, I discovered eight messages from Kevin, three from Emily and one from the principal of my school. I had become so engrossed in Momma's story, I didn't even hear the tones on my telephone. I answered each message on my hurried walk back to the house where I fixed a quick dinner and gave Honey a break.

That night, after helping Momma to bed, I leafed through the first scrapbook. It was filled with drawings of birds and trees, and a rather good head shot in pencil of a young boy with serious eyes and mouth and dark hair. Under it, with hearts drawn all along the sides like a frame (like young girls do) were the words, "Callaway Thompson." I smiled, thinking of all the years and difficulties their love had endured. Even now, 70 years after she met him, my mother's eyes turned sparkly when she talked about him. After his death four years ago, she still called for him in the night and turned looking for his arms to hold her as she slept.

When I thought about Steve, it wasn't with the rush of emotions I wanted to feel. Now, it was almost like I tried not to think about him, it just upset me. I hated when I felt that way, when I had needed him he had been supportive and caring, but now, maybe I just didn't need him anymore. I couldn't imagine calling for him, or turning to him in the night. We slept far apart from each other in the bed, unless he wanted sex, of course, then he would touch me. But, afterward we turned away from each other and slept in our own personal dreams. *Is this the way love is nowadays?* I really couldn't think of any of my friends who shared the same kind of love my parents did. Momma and Daddy spent time together, doing things together every day. If the house needed cleaning, he helped. If the chicken coop needed a new roof, she helped. In their later years, they bought a second hand RV and traveled together until the year he died. Always, they talked and laughed together. Sure, they argued, both were hot headed, but they never went to bed angry, never held a grudge. They were truly best friends.

Most of my friends, and us included, took separate vacations now – a golf trip for a week for the men, time on the beach or shopping in Gatlinburg for the women. I hated to go anywhere with Steve anymore, he didn't like to fly, he said it was too expensive, so we drove wherever it was we were going. Usually, we went to the same place and did the same things. I wanted to go to Maine and Vermont and do an entire tour of the east coast, he said it was too cold. We would end up at Daytona Beach in a one bedroom condo, close to where his cousins lived and eat at the same restaurants and visit them and stay in the condo most of the time while he watched baseball and slept on the couch and I read or took long walks on the beach. In the car, he would tune the radio to baseball games, or listen to 70's rock and roll (the only kind of music I didn't like) and I would download books on my Kindle and read two or three. Mostly silence reined between us, we never could seem to find a topic to discuss.

I reached over and grabbed the next journal in the pile and opened it, ready to escape my own thoughts and learn more about the lady, I called Momma.

CHAPTER THIRTEEN:

Sarah

It was Aug 13th 1953. Sara dreaded walking through the high school door for the first time. She was newly 15 and starting school. She heard so many horror stories of the bullies there, she feared, as always, that she would be singled out. Even though it was 1953, most people she knew held tight to their prejudices and still looked down on her. The only people who didn't were Colton, Callaway and Natalie the Nurse Midwife, and there was something about the way Colton looked at her lately that really made her mistrust him. Natalie had told her to listen to her instincts, "God gave women a certain gift to feel the nature of a man. If you feel that there is something wrong, listen to your heart, stay away."

She and Natalie had become close friends, despite their age difference. She made a habit of visiting every day she could and if Natalie didn't have a patient to see, or a birth to attend, they would sit on the front porch and drink sweet tea and talk about everything under the sun. Natalie was encouraging her to think about going to college, something Sarah had never considered before. She had told her about the college where she went to get her nursing degree, Berea College. The people there only accepted poor children and didn't charge tuition – each student received a job that benefited the others on campus and they worked for their tuition and room and board. No one cared about color there, or if she was part Indian, it was a college originally founded to educate blacks and whites together, now since the Day Law was in effect, it focused on educating Appalachian students – girls and boys and helping them rise above the poverty they were raised in. It sounded like Heaven to Sarah.

Sarah knew all about poverty. Her father had been sick for about eight months and, Natalie said, he would not get any better. Honey did everything she could to keep the family fed and together. She sold eggs, took in wash, and cleaned other people's houses. The children contributed as much as they could, the boys kept the gardens going for food, they were just not able to take care of the larger money crops, Father and Honey both decreed they were to stay in school no matter what, so they would hire out to other farmers on the weekends and during breaks from school. Sarah would come home after school and clean the house and make dinner, her younger sisters would help. But, there were times when they sat down for supper and all of them almost fell asleep into their meal. During the summer, she worked in the garden and barns, milking the cow, the horse was long gone, and caring for the chickens and turkeys. The boys would come home long after sunset and eat in exhausted silence, smile at her then wash and go straight to bed. It was a hard life for them all. At least, though, they were together.

Early in the spring, Sarah walked into the kitchen to find Honey in tears. Honey never cried, she always kept a smile on her face, seeing her sitting at the table with a dish towel up to her face sobbing frightened Sarah, "Oh my god, is Daddy dead?" she questioned.

"No, it's worse! The cow didn't have any milk this morning. All I have in the pantry is green beans and dill pickles. My favorite chicken was dead when I went out to get the eggs and now Mr Teague wants toast and scrambled eggs and I don't have bread nor eggs!" Honey kept sobbing into the towel. I'm doing the best I can, I swear, but I can't take care of you all."

"Do we have anything else?" Sarah asked.

"We have some biscuits I cooked yesterday, and a ham hock. How am I supposed to feed you kids?"

"Looks like we are having green beans and dill pickles. We'll figure out something." Sarah went to the pantry and found a jar of applesauce squeezed back into the pantry behind all the
205

empty jars waiting for summer. "Hey, look! Applesauce!" she shouted.

Honey jumped up, "I have an idea!" She took the applesauce and dumped it into a large pot and added the last little bit of butter and some water to it. Then she turned up the flame until it came to a slow boil. She took the leftover biscuits and tore them into tiny bites and dropped them into the applesauce and cooked it down into a mushlike consistency. "There," she said, "We are having applesauce dumplings for breakfast!" She smiled a big smile. Tonight we will have ham surprise, if you can find ham in the green beans, it will be a surprise!" Her grin faded as she looked at Sarah, "we have to do something, Sarah. I don't want you to leave school, but we have to feed the kids."

"I know someone I can talk to," said Sarah thinking of how Callaway's family didn't take welfare and he and Colton were big and strong. "Maybe he can help."

That day at school, she nervously waited for Callaway at the door. Right before the bell rang, he came rushing in with his group of friends and, seeing Sarah, he told them all to go ahead. He walked over to where she stood against the wall and leaned his arm up beside her, "Hey, Redskin, whatcha need?"

She smiled at him, only Callaway could call her that because she knew he didn't mean it. "I need help." As she told him about the food situation, he straightened up.

"There's lots of food right now," he protested. Just go out in the woods.

"Well, obviously if I knew what I was looking for, I would," she replied with some heat. I'd get poisonous berries and toadstools, Callaway, I don't even know what to look for. Please, can you come help us?"

"I'll be there tomorrow. I need you and Martha and the oldest boys ready at dawn. Keep the kids home."

"Thank you," she answered a bit embarrassed she lost her temper.

As he walked away, he turned and looked at her over his shoulder. With his blue eyes sparkling he commented, "Hey, Sarah?"

"Hey what?" she answered.

"You sure are cute when you are all heated up." He laughed at her blush and continued on to first period class.

Sarah was late to a class for the first time in her life, but she entered Home Ec with a grin on her face.

Callaway, true to his word, arrived at their door very early the next morning. He carried a rifle and a large burlap bag with him. First, he went in to talk to her father for a few minutes, then when he came out, he was carrying her father's gun. He asked Sarah and Martha to grab four sacks and Matthew and Thomas to find the box of ammunition under their bed. "I know y'all got some gardens here and such, but I want to take you out and show you some other stuff.

Times are hard 'n I want you all to take care of yerselves."

So, he took them deep into the woods. He gave Thomas his gun and Matthew used Father's. "Your father tells me you boys are decent shots. I want you to sit here and be quiet. This is a good spot for bucks. Only shoot a buck, it's a sin to shoot a new Mamma Deer. The girls and me are going to be out by the pond, don't shoot us."

He took the girls by the pond and showed them the fresh greens they could eat, "Ain't nothing like poke salad with a bit of bacon grease and vinegar on top," he assured them. Then they searched for the brainlike morel mushrooms. Finally, he found a bunch of pansies all around an old farmstead. "These will help make your salad taste even better."

He showed them how to make a fishing pole and they caught three bluegill and two crappie while they were waiting to hear a gunshot. Eventually, they did and he left the girls at the pond to go help the boys gut and clean the deer they got.

When they returned to the pond to get the girls' and their treasure, Sarah noticed that all three boys seemed upset. "What happened?" she questioned.

"Thomas got excited and shot the first deer he saw," answered Callaway. "It was a pregnant doe. I tried to tell him it would be ok, but he knows it's bad to kill a mother."

Sarah walked over beside Thomas who was trying hard to stifle his tears. "It's ok, Brother," and put her arm around him.

"No, it's not. Callaway said it was a sin, and now the preacher's gonna call me in front of the church and I'm gonna go to hell!" he cried.

Callaway took the girls and Matthew, with their bags and the deer carcass on ahead so Sarah could keep talking to Thomas.

"I tell you what, that preacher's god doesn't care about our land or animals," she told Thomas as she guided him to a fallen tree trunk to sit.

"That god only cares about punishing and sending people to hell. We don't like him. But, if you read the Bible on your own, that's a different god. Remember, it's says He loves us so much He sent us His son to die in our place. That's pretty cool. I like that god better. Plus it says that if we say we're sorry and mean it, that He will take our sins and cast them from the east to the west and remember them no more. That's a long way away, the east from the west, and if He doesn't remember, then we should be ok. Maybe we can just sit here and tell god you're sorry. He sees in your heart and knows."

Thomas said a small prayer, "Sister, if I'm really sorry I wouldn't eat the deer, right?"

"No, I don't think so. I think it's a sign of respect to the deer to be thankful and to use the life she gave in a good way. This meat is going to keep you, and us, strong and healthy. We can sell the hide for some extra money. We needed it, Thomas. Maybe that's why she stepped out in front of you."

Thomas nodded his head. "OK, I need to go help Callaway prepare it." Suddenly, he leaned over and hugged her tight, "I love you, Sarah." And he ran off after the others.

That night they dined on deer roast with a rich gravy. Honey had cleaned house that day for Natalie and instead of asking for money asked for carrots and potatoes. Natalie also gave her some jars of tomatoes and okra. It felt like a feast, roast, carrots, potatoes and mushrooms all cooked together in the iron pot over the fire with poke salad and pansies on the side. They ate until they couldn't take another bite. Honey took the leftover and added a jar of tomatoes and turned it into a tasty venison stew for the next day's lunch.

All the kids and Honey pitched in to butcher and save the deer and the fetus. Callaway skinned both and sold them to a man he knew. He brought the money to Honey, but refused any share. She used it to buy some sugar and flour at the store.

Every weekend after that, Callaway came and took the kids by the ponds and the roadsides and even their own lawn. He showed them the grass that he called wheatgrass and when they tasted it, it was sweet. He taught them how to dig the onion spring ramps. He showed them how to gather cattails, what parts to eat, especially the nutritious pollen. He showed them how to set traps for small animals, and how to skin them and butcher them. He pointed out all the edible roots and leaves and berries, even the trees that would grow nuts and fruit. Between the knowledge he gave them and their gardens, they never grew hungry again, or even wanted for variety, there was always an abundance of food. Callaway would say, "I reckon God had to put food here for us not to starve, we just gotta be smart enough to know what it is. And don't forget to give thanks for it."

Lavani

I smiled at the memories of my daddy this brought back to me. He loved the land and all it gave. He didn't go to church much, but when Momma or the preacher pressured him he'd say, "I go to God all day every day. I see sights more beautiful than any church could build and I give thanks in my own way. I don't need hymns and long prayers there to give my word of thanks and awe here. God knows where I am, me and him, we're ok." What a profound statement that was, I wished I was ok with God.

Sarah

There was no hunger in their house, but their poverty screamed in different ways. It was hard to find the money for fabric to make clothes and they came to rely upon the clothes sent from Mount Mission. These clothes were ill fitting and out of style, or faded and in strange colors. But, they were clean and warm and her family had learned to make do. She might not wear poodle skirts and sweater sets to school, but she would wear a couple of skirts together to make them look fuller and an old white dress shirt of her father's with the tail out. She would tie her hair back with a "scarf" made from her sister's ripped pink blouse, and pretend to herself that she looked the same as the other girls. She really tried not to care that she was not only a different color, but she dressed differently. She didn't even like these girls who teased who for her lack of nice things, but she wanted to be like them. Natalie and Honey both said she was just being "typical girl" and they all went through it, but Sarah felt selfish and small.

She was especially ashamed of herself for the fit she had thrown when it had come time for 8th grade graduation. All the other girls in her school were talking about the long white dresses they had gone to town to buy. They were describing the small rows of lace ruffles and the wide sashes they would wear, the long white gloves and the beehive style they planned for their hair. She knew all she could wear was the long white dress they had found in the bottom of the pile at the Mission. It just fell straight to the floor, no ruffles no crinoline, with a high neck and long sleeves. It was hot and itchy and fit her petite curvaceousness in all the wrong places, making her look like a child parading around in an adult's dress. But the requirement was a long white dress and it was all she had.

One night, after a long day of tests and teasing, she went up to her room and saw it hanging, neatly pressed in her room. She jerked it off the hanger and threw it on the bed, crying. Honey came in and watched her as she put it on the bed and punched it with her fists, crying, "I hate this dress. I hate it I hate it! I hate being poor, I just want nice things and to be normal! I want blonde hair and blue eyes and just, for once, for someone to like me – just for me!" She could hear herself, but she couldn't stop the raging ugly words that escaped her.

Honey had listened in silence, then just wrapped her arms around her and told her, "I love you just for you." Sarah turned into her arms and sobbed on her shoulder until the tears would no longer came. Then Honey helped her to bed and hung up her dress. Sarah laid in bed, horrified at the things she'd said, especially when she remembered Honey didn't even have the chance to go to school at all. All she did was work and take care of kids and a sick husband, the only learning she had was the few hours she would study with the kids at the kitchen table at night. They had taught her how to read and she had a love for it, but seldom was able to get new books to read.

When she woke the next morning, she went straight to Honey, "I'm sorry. I'm sorry I'm so selfish. I want you to know I love you." That day at the library, she checked out two books she knew Honey would love and left them on the kitchen table that night. It was a small peace offering, but all she could do.

The night of 8th grade graduation came and Natalie came over to help Honey get everyone ready for the ceremony. The boys were wearing nicely pressed jeans with the holes carefully patched and the girls were in pretty spring dresses that mostly fit. Honey and Natalie worked on Sarah's hair and only let her see it when they were finished. When they turned her around she was speechless. Earlier in the mirror, a half grown girl with dark brown eyes and long black hair pulled back into a braid had looked back at her. Now, she looked like a young lady. The tops and sides of her hair had been teased into a tall dome on top of her head and they had cut little bangs to frame her face. The rest of it lay curled in long sausage curls that Natalie had teased a little to make them look a little messy. Her face, for the first time in her life wore make up. Her eyes were lined with a black eyeliner on the top and the bottom and her lashes were long and dark with the mascara Natalie had brought with her. They had colored her lids with a lighter shade and shaped her rather bushy eyebrows into high arches. Her mouth, currently hanging open in shock, was coated with a bright red lipstick. "Wow," Natalie said, "you look like a pin-up girl!"

Sarah was so excited about getting to wear make-up that she decided not to complain about her ugly dress. Honey, drew her away from the mirror when it was time to put it on, "Sarah, we made a few changes to your graduation dress, we want to surprise you." They had her turn her back to the mirror and slip off her robe, underneath she had on her slip, pantyhose and her first pair of high heels only one size too big, borrowed from Natalie. They positioned the

219

dress under her and had her step into it with her eyes closed. Sarah tried to pretend that it didn't itch, that it would feel smooth against her skin and flare out from her hips, she worked so hard at it that she convinced herself that's exactly how it felt. They zipped up the back and had her put on the long white gloves (again borrowed from Natalie) and then turned her toward the mirror. "Open your eyes!"

Sarah opened her eyes, expecting to see the Mission dress, instead her mouth dropped open. She was wearing a white dress and that's where the similarity ended. This dress was beautiful! It had a boat neckline lined in white lace and a tight bodice with a wide white sash around her waist. The dress fell from her waist in tiny tiers of white lace all the way to her feet, each tier a little bit fuller than the last. It was the most gorgeous dress she had ever seen. "How? Why?" She couldn't even form the questions.

Natalie and Honey's faces shone with grins in the mirror beside her. "My niece graduated from 8th grade last year. When I told her about your dress, she said she had just the answer. This is the dress, shoes and gloves she wore. It's too small for her now, she took a big growth spurt, so she said you could have it."

Sarah's eyes filled with tears, "Oh oh it's too much!

Natalie responded, "No, it's not. It would have just hung in the back of her closet. It would be a shame to let this dress just fade and rot. It needs to be worn. She and my sister were both glad to be able to send it. They sent a bunch of other stuff for you girls too, but you can look through that tomorrow."

That night, Sarah was the Belle of the Ball. When she walked in, the girls and boys of her class had to look twice to recognize her. Her teachers were so impressed, they forgot that she was a "half breed" and talked to her and told her she looked pretty. After the graduation ceremony, Father insisted they all go to the diner in town. There he bought small bowls of ice cream for them, he had his own, Honey and Sarah shared one, Thomas and Matthew shared one, Elizabeth and John shared one and Ruth and Martha shared. It was a perfect night. When they entered the diner, everyone had stopped talking and stared, but this time in a good way. She wished it never had to end.

Lavani

I put down the journal, "I remember that dress, I've seen it!" First, I checked up on Momma, sleeping in her bedroom with Honey crocheting in the chair beside her. "Honey, I'm running to the attic," I told her then ran up the steps into the dark attic. I walked over to a large cedar box under the window and opened it. Inside, I found pretty amazing treasures: metal cars and trucks my brother must have played with, a doll (barely used) given to me by an aunt who never understood I was a tomboy, and a Barbie doll head of my sister's. I found our graduation caps and gowns and lots of scrapbooks. Near the bottom, I found the dress I searched for, wrapped in tissue paper and carefully folded. Gently pulling it from its nest, I held it up, admiring the intricacy of the lace work and the marveling at the tiny waist. Scrapbooks downstairs showcased pictures of Momma and Aunt Martha both wearing this dress. Momma looked gorgeous in it, like a tiny china doll. Being thankful for the people who understood that a young girl, especially one already mistreated because of her appearance, would need a beautiful dress to shine on a special day made the dress even more beautiful.

Vaguely, I remembered "Aunt" Natalie as a short, kind of dumpy woman with grey hair and the wrinkles that said she spent a great deal of time in the sun. She passed away when I was young, in fact, her funeral stuck as one of my first memories. Natalie must have been an incredible reader of human nature. No wonder Momma had loved her so much she followed into her footsteps and entered the nurse midwifery program. I hugged the dress to me, then carefully refolded it and put it back into the chest followed by the usual remembrances of a family, the toys and report cards, love notes and mother's day cards. It was a treasure trove to us.

223

CHAPTER FOURTEEN:

Isn't it funny what mothers keep? After I neatly repacked Momma's trunk, I sat on the attic floor, thinking about the objects that hold so many precious memories to mothers, are absolutely not worth anything on the open market, and we like it that way. I thought about my own treasure trove at home, in an old steamer trunk in the basement, all put away in space saver bags and boxes. Emily's bag bulged with dance costumes, archery gloves, marching band hats and her high school cap and gown. Next to it lay a box of papers and drawings from the time she struggled to hold a crayon until the one she had brought me recently of a sketch she made of the scenery from my front porch. She framed it through the front door and showed my profile while I sat on the swing, drinking coffee, looking out at the yard. She captured my favorite little dog, a miniature dachshund in my lap, who

227

died years ago. The portrait was beautiful with the detailing and the fact that she knew my favorite spot; yet, I remembered a feeling of repulsion almost. Who was that old woman with shadings of gray in her hair and sorrow in her face? The thing I treasured most in her side of that trunk was her "baby blanket". It used to be a light blue with pictures of precious moments children on it, faded now with scraggly threads on the edges where the stitches came through. The middle of it looked worn, almost transparent, but it still felt soft and warm. I hoped it waited for another child to drag it through life's adventures. I couldn't wait to give it back to her when she had a baby.

Christian's side looked much the same. I stuffed it with treasures: boxes of notes and report cards, drawings, and certificates, his box of trophies and old toys we just couldn't bear to get rid of, and his space saver bag that held his old jerseys, his high school baseball and golf team jerseys, the shirt he umpired in, the blanket that was on his bed the day he died and his stuffed clown. I remembered the day I found that clown a few months after he passed away, and

228

the decision to put Clown in the bag; I kept explaining to Christian in my mind that I was not putting him away, I was trying to keep him safe and special. I don't know if I was trying to convince his spirit, or me.

When Christian was very young, maybe five, I heard him giggling in his room. He often did that in his sleep, and I went to investigate the joke. At some point I told him that angels told him jokes in his ear at night, he thought that was great and would ask me when I tucked him in if they were coming that night. This night, I had fussed at him a little over his room, he was such a slob, and told him he had to clean it the next day, so he went to bed pouting. But, he still leaned over and kissed me. "Best boy, ever," I said like every night, until the day I lost him.

"Best Momma, ever," he replied then smiled at me as I tucked him safely in under the blankets. "Will the angels come, tonight, Momma?"

"Maybe, if they aren't busy keeping kids safe and helping others."

"I like it when they do, I have good dreams."

"I know, Baby Boy. Good night sleep time."

He turned over and fell asleep and was still sleeping soundly now, even after laughing. His night light was on so I could see that Clown was lying on the floor. I quietly stepped over the toys and clothes on his floor, if Christian woke up and couldn't find Clown, I'd be in there looking anyway. I found the stuffed creature under the bed and put it back in Christian's arms. Startled, I saw that his eyes were wide open.

"Thanks, Mom, you got my back!" His new favorite phrase.

"Yep, I have your back, your front and your sides," I whisper as I kiss his forehead, his cheeks and his chin, "and don't you forget it."

Smiling at the sweetest of memories, I finished putting Momma's treasures back into the chest and went downstairs to check on what she and Honey needed me to do. I dreamed of Christian that night. Dreams are rare and far between for me, so each one is treasured. I was in labor, transitional and Pitocin enhanced. I hurt horribly all through my body and I was just trying to breathe chee cheee hooo, chee chee hoo; suddenly I was pulled up out of the bed by my arms, then pulled upright into a floor above. There, my son wrapped both arms around my waist, I wrapped both around his chest and we just held tightly to each other for a long long time. We didn't speak, just hugged. I didn't want to wake up, but I did, I drifted back into my bed and woke up peacefully. Of course, I cried, but this time there was some comfort in the tears.

I spent the next day caring for Momma. She had several episodes that day, including one that involved Kevin. He stopped by to visit her and see if we needed anything. In the middle of dinner, she became very confused and starting talking to him as if he was Daddy. She kept reaching for his hand. Finally, he just leaned over and held her hand in his.

"Oh, Callaway, I've missed you so much," she said.

"I know. I've missed you too," Kevin just fell into the role.

"I love you. I want you here with me. I'm tired of you being gone," she stated, petulantly.

"I love you, too. It won't be long until we are together again," he reassured her.

Eventually, she leaned her head back on her chair and fell asleep, still holding Kevin's hand. He got up from the table and picked her up in his arms and carried her to her room. I rushed ahead of him to get the bed ready. After he laid her on the bed, he sat beside her just holding her hand for a long time. I went into the kitchen and cleaned up the dishes.

Finally, I stepped outside to the porch and sat on the swing. After a few minutes Kevin joined me. "I put some iced tea for you on the table," I told him.

He sat beside me on the swing, uncharacteristically silent. He reached over and held my hand for the first time in twenty years. We swung for several minutes as we held hands and he rubbed his thumb in circles over my thumb and hand. I thought about all the times we did this while we were dating, and how good it felt. "I've always wanted that kind of love," he said, breaking our silence. "They were married so long, yet always seemed to want to be together. I want that. I want to know that when I'm gone, my love will still want me."

"I know what you mean," I replied. We moved back and forth, enjoying the evening air. I turned to tell him something, when he laid his hand on my face and kissed me. His lips felt so soft against mine, his hand lay warm on my cheek. We kissed for a long time, one kiss leading to another and another, until I laid my head on his shoulder. I found tears running down my face, it felt so natural to kiss him and feel his hand on my cheek. Eventually, he got up from the swing and after one last sweet kiss, he walked out to his truck. I watched him drive away and wondered what this meant. I kissed a man other than my husband for the first time in twenty-five years, and I didn't feel guilty.

I almost floated back into the house and to my room, truly thankful Honey slept already. I knew it would be a while before I could sleep, so I opened Momma's journal and started reading again.

CHAPTER FIFTEEN:

Sarah

The first few weeks of high school replicated all of grade school. Students and teachers spoke to Sarah, only if necessary "Excuse me, Do you have your homework?" the kind of comments, always directed her way. The night of the beautiful dress seemed wiped out of everyone's memories but her own. On the other hand, no one treated her badly. The cushion created by Colton and Callaway in grade school still held. She would see them, the twins, in the hallways, in the lunchroom or the gym and they appeared to always be laughing. Colton the star of the football team, fought viciously on the field, the rumors said he tried to break the bones of other players just to see if he could. Callaway played first baseman and clean-up batter on the school team. He remained cool in the face of any situation. They dated the prettiest girls, the cheerleaders (rah rah girls as Sarah thought of them) and the popular ones who always stood in the hall discussing make up and dates and whether or not to have sex and how far to go. The girls would sneak into the bathroom and light up cigarettes and practice blowing smoke through their mouths and noses and gossip about boys and cheer leading and the upcoming dance or pep rally. They pretended they didn't even see her when she entered the stall then came out and washed her hands. It was so hard to be invisible, but better than to be mistreated. Sarah missed the days that Callaway would say he was marrying her, but just kept pushing through each day as it came, knowing that she was one day closer to her dream of being a nurse midwife.

At lunch one day, she sat down and put her bag on her usual table in the lunchroom. She opened her novel and started to read (as she always did). "Excuse me, may I please sit down? Ummm, hello? Can I sit down?" Surely there wasn't anyone asking to sit with her! Startled she looked up from her book at a decidedly annoyed redhead standing beside the table, "Can.

I. Sit. Down?" The girl asked as if Sarah was really stupid.

"Uh, of course," she stammered, "sure."

The girl sat and immediately started talking, she spoke so fast and pushed her words so close together Sarah leaned toward her to understand what she said, "My name is Molly. We just moved here from New York, my parents and me. Today's my first day. I'm a freshman and I hate it here already. Who are you?"

"I … I.. " she stammered, then blushed, she just wasn't used to talking to girls her age. "I'm Sarah," she finally managed.

"God, are you one of those dumb Appalachians too?" Molly sputtered, "I only sat here because I saw you reading *Jane Eyre* and I love that book and I thought maybe I could have a conversation with someone with some sense."

"No, I'm not stupid," Sarah replied with some heat, "I'm just not used to sitting with anyone, that's all."

"Oh, is it because you are Indian? I've never had an Indian friend."

Sarah gaped at her, no one ever mentioned her heritage, at least not in a casual way from a complete stranger. She realized it felt good, to lay that out in the open, "Yeah, it's because I'm an Indian, I guess they are afraid I'm going to scalp them. Be warned, you have some pretty red hair." She held her breath, hoping she hadn't said too much, gone too far.

Molly just leaned her head back and laughed so loudly some of the kids at the next table looked up startled. "Well you can have the red hair, I hate it. Take these green eyes and freckles, too, will you? You look beautiful and exotic, I just look Irish." She took out her class schedule and they discovered they shared all but one class. Molly played in band and Sarah took art. "Swell," Molly said, "Can you show me where I'm going then? I've been late to every class and everyone stares at me. The bell rang signaling the end of the lunch period and they both stood, Molly, at five foot nine, towered over

Sarah's five feet, "Well, damn, you do have to be petite and cute too, don't you?" Molly said.

"Well, you are tall and elegant," Sarah said back. They smiled at each other and it became the beginning of the first friendship with a girl her age Sarah ever had. Sarah and Molly became inseparable after that. Molly's parents were missionaries sent to "SAVE THE MOUNTAIN PEOPLE" as Molly would always explain it then giggle. They owned the only store in town. They sold everything from flour to soap, to fabric to magazines. Some days after school, when the chores were not waiting at home, they would go to the store and carefully remove one of the magazines from the rack and sneak it upstairs to Molly's room. There, they would look at the pictures of the women in the gorgeous dresses and beehives and talk about leaving that town and going out into the world. They were careful not to bend any pages and would return the magazine before Molly's dad noticed it missing. Molly decided to be a singer and famous and Sarah determined to be a nurse midwife, no matter how many times Molly tried to talk her into forming an all-girl band. They would lay on her bed and listen to records and sing along with hairbrushes as microphones. They did each other's make up and fixed each other's hair and tried their first cigarettes together. Both decided they wouldn't smoke and they wouldn't have sex until they married, but they would allow a boy to reach second base. It was a magical time for Sarah.

Lavani

I smiled as I read the entries detailing Momma's experiences with Molly. It reminded me of all the good times growing up with my best friend, Patti. Patti and Kevin spent so much time on the farm with me, that my momma joked she had other children. We laughed and knew they were as welcome as us. She stayed with us so much that Daddy used to pretend to write her bills for the food and bed; one time, Patti paid with Monopoly money.

I lost touch with Patti after I married Steve. She and Jayce stood with me, but both argued I should stay single and raise the baby on my own, instead. She never liked Steve, and after Christian was born and diagnosed, I didn't have the time to put an effort into friendship. I heard that she married after college, and they lived here in town with three half grown kids. My Momma kept me informed about every time they ran into each other, but secondhand news never maintained a relationship. I missed her, too.

I imagined my lips still tingled from Kevin's kisses, so rather than trying to go back to sleep, I checked on Momma and then turned back to her journals.

Sarah

Even on the days she had to go home and work in the house and cook dinner, she would bring home a note with her from Molly and read it over and over, just to think about her friend. A few times Molly came home with her. She helped, fascinated, by the process of milking the cow. Sarah showed her over and over how to hold her hands just right. The old cow stood patiently while they giggled and gossiped more than they worked. Molly refused to go into the Chicken Coop though, "That just stinks, Indian," she'd say. But she stood outside the fence and talked to Sarah as she gathered eggs, cleaned up what needed cleaning and fed the birds. Sometimes, after they finished the chores, Sarah took her a little way into the woods and tried to teach her the things Callaway had taught her about the seeds and weeds and trees, but Molly laughed, "I bet they don't have any of that in Hollywood! Besides, I get what I need from a store like normal people." Some of her comments sounded harsh, but Sarah knew that was just her personality. She knew Molly had taken up for her on more than one occasion and had lost any chance of other friends because of hanging out with her.

Sarah had been called to the office to check out one of the younger sisters, Martha, who had fallen and scraped her arm. She cleaned it and kissed it and sent her back to class. As she entered into her math class right before the bell rang, she saw a girl talking to Molly and then Molly's face turn bright red as she sat down into her desk. "What's wrong?" she asked as the bell rang.

"Nothing," Molly muttered. "Stupid Bitch."

"What???"

"Oh not you, the rah rah girl. She's a stupid bitch." And she glared at the girl, like she wanted to burn the perky ponytail right off her head.

243

The teacher quieted the class, but Sarah couldn't concentrate and kept getting the answers wrong. Afterward, she and Molly walked to their lockers in silence. As the cheerleader who talked to Molly earlier passed them she said, "Stupid Irish Indian Lover," then laughed and waved at her squad. She spoke loudly as she stepped up to them, "Look at those animals pretending to be human, an Indian and her Indian loving Yankee." The rest of the girls giggled and looked at them, waiting for their reactions.

Sarah felt tears in her eyes, the first in a long time, "I'm sorry," she strangled out, "I'm sorry, Molly."

Molly stared at her, then started yelling, "Why are YOU sorry? YOU are SORRY they are too stupid and ignorant to know the color of the skin doesn't matter? You are SORRY they are just little hick town girls who are going to marry hick town boys and have lots of hillbilly babies and get fat and toothless?? YOU are sorry? Let me tell you something, where I come from it's those girls who would get teased for their country accents and the words they use."

She pointed at the group with great force, as if she could poke through them, "They'd be made fun of from the time they get up until the time they go to bed. They think they are so great and wonderful, but they are ugly inside and out and they don't even know I wore their stylish clothes two years before they could get them in a store! They should be the SORRY ones, not you." With that, she tossed her hair, sneered at the group of suddenly silent girls and said in a fake mountain drawl, "Y'all ain't nothin' but white trash mountain scum, too ignert to know yer hillbillies and hicks. Y'all ain't ever gonna be nothin' and ever gonna do nothin' but have hillbilly babies and get fat and get the welfare check!" and she walked quickly down the hall out the door and into town.

Sarah just stared after her, "Wow," she whispered, then threw back her head and went after her friend. Not one girl other than Sarah spoke to Molly after that, but the under the breath comments stopped too, and Molly said that was better. Sarah just felt thankful that Molly chose to be friends with her.

Lavani

I was impressed with this Molly girl; but, also, confused; why had I never heard about her? If such a good friend of Momma's lived close by, wouldn't I have met her at some point? Or heard of her? I decided to ask Honey.

That next afternoon, while Momma napped in the swing, Honey and I shucked corn on the porch so I asked, "Who is Molly?"

Honey just looked at me for a few minutes, "Oh, it's a long sad story," she said.

"I'd really like to hear it." I insisted.

Make me a cup of tea, and I will tell you, she promised. Sensing she needed the time to gather

her thoughts, I hurried into the kitchen and put the tea pot on the stove. When I returned to the porch, Honey had cleaned the mess of the corn shucking away and begun to silk the pile with her hand brush. I set the tea on the table beside her and took my seat again. Grabbing my brush, I picked up one of the corn cobs and began to silk.

Honey took a deep breath, "I never wanted to think about that sweet girl going through such bad times, again," she said. "But, it's important for you to know, and I guess remembering her honors her memory."

Honey

"Sarah turned sixteen and started dating Callaway. He had dated other girls while waiting for her, but he was the only boy who had ever asked her out. She had just lost her father about six months before and I had met my soon to be husband, in fact, we tried to double date once,

247

but that was just weird, besides, one of us had to be home to watch the kids and we worried the whole time the house would be gone when we got home." Honey chuckled as she leaned back in her rocking chair. "It was the Sadie Hawkins dance and Sarah had worked up the courage to ask Callaway and talked Molly into asking Colton, he accepted and they had a great time. Colton was on his best behavior and Callaway and Sarah were always fun to be around and Molly just fell head over heels for Colton. They all became quite the item to see around town. Two very handsome boys, your beautiful Momma and the tall striking red head.

I don't think it took very long until Colton started being unkind to Molly. I think that boy had something warped in him from the very beginning; he seemed to like to cause trouble and pain wherever he went. Molly started losing weight, she wore long sleeves or sweaters most of the time, just saying she was cold, and she lost that special exuberance we knew her for. We were all pretty worried. Sarah and I both nagged her to tell us what was wrong, but she just wouldn't open up.

Then came the day that Callaway came to tell Sarah he was enlisting and going away to war. She was devastated! He felt like he needed to serve his country and also this was a way to earn some money to buy a farm to have for her and their family someday. She felt like he needed to stay home and be safe, that would be taking better care of their family, but you know men, if the trumpets of war sound, they gonna march. Anyway, she and Callaway were fighting about that and Molly was drifting farther and farther away. It was a bad time. The only thing that made that time sweet was that Leonard had asked me to marry him, and he wanted to raise the kids. We were planning a wedding and I had asked Sarah to be my maid of honor. Your aunts were my bridesmaids and your uncles were the groomsmen. It was perfect for me, I'd never had anyone who loved me like Leonard did, and I was going to be a bride." She smiled in that way women have when they think about their first true love. I smiled back at her, but remained silent so she could continue her story.

"Anyway, back to Molly. She was pulling away and Sarah was scared and angry at Callaway. He had left for Korea at this point and the only way they could communicate was through letters, they are in that pile of stuff your mom gave you, I think."

I nodded, I had seen a large stack of envelopes wrapped in a faded yellow ribbon.

"Sarah was a senior by this time and she was busy applying to Berea College, we knew that was her only chance of getting educated. Molly had quit talking about doing anything after school, she was just, you know, listless.

One day Sarah said something to her and when Molly didn't hear, she grabbed her arm to get her attention. Molly flinched away in pain. Sarah grabbed her sweater and pulled up her sleeve, her arm was just covered in bruises. From her wrist to her elbow, finger sized bruises ran up and down her arms. Sarah brought her home to me, and we called Natalie. She took her into Sarah's bedroom and made her show all of her injuries, and there were a lot. Not only that, the poor girl was about four months pregnant. We were all stunned. Sarah cried and begged for forgiveness, but Molly just told her that it was fine, she wouldn't have told her anyway. Her mother had just figured out she was pregnant a week before and they had made a plan to save her reputation.

She and her mother were going to go visit relatives in New York when Sarah started showing. Before that, her mother would confide to a few friends that she was going to visit her relatives in New York and stay with them so that she could seek better pregnancy care since her last birth had been so difficult. Molly was going with her to help her out when she needed it. When they came back in a few months, Molly would have a new "sister or brother" and her mother would have a new child. No one would ever find out the baby was Molly's."

Honey laughed at the look of shock on my face. "Oh Darling, now you know sex wasn't invented by your generation. This wasn't an uncommon occurrence really. It saved face all the way around. The worst part of it all would be that Molly would have to drop out of school. She claimed she didn't care, but we all knew she did. After we discovered the extent of Colton's abuse, we called Molly's mother and she came right over. We sat at that kitchen table and decided how to best protect Molly; we knew the Sheriff wouldn't mess with Colton, his son was one of the football cronies Colton hung out with. Besides, Colton had a reputation for being hard and mean by then. He was working at the saw mill, drinking, and getting in fights with the immigrants. Rumor had it he stole from them when they were paid, if they complained, he just beat them down. Molly's mother said she could have everything ready to go in a week, and they were going to go on and leave town a couple of months earlier than planned and then Molly could stay with her parents in New York when she came back and just start off fresh again. It wasn't a great plan, probably, but it was the best they had."

Honey paused and leaned her head back in the rocker for a while. I went to the kitchen and got her a cup of tea, so many questions were racing through my mind that I didn't even know where to start. I set the tea beside her, "So, Molly is living in New York? Did she ever become an actress or singer?" Neither of us realized Momma lay awake listening until she took over the story.

Sarah

"No, she never did. She never made it to New York. We aren't sure how Colton found out, probably from the ticket master at the train station, but he discovered that Molly was leaving. One day after school, he was waiting for her at the door. She smiled at him, like nothing was happening but he grabbed her by the arm. I stayed at her side trying to talk to him, to get him to let go of Molly so she could run; but, he didn't listen. He drug her into the alley between the bar and the Methodist Church and started yelling at her terrible things. He kept saying she was his property and he wasn't going to let her go. I got between them and yelled for Molly to run, but Molly wouldn't leave me." By this time tears streaked down Momma's face, "He punched me in the side of the head and I blacked out for a little bit. When I came to, God, Molly was on the ground and Colton was kicking her in the side. He just kept kicking her." I forced myself up and screamed, praying that someone would hear me and come help, then jumped on Colton's back and pounded as hard I could on his face and head, I didn't even know what I was doing, I just knew I had to keep him from Molly. He fell backwards into the bar's wall knocking me off of him, then punched me in the face again. He probably would have hurt me more, but ran when he heard some people coming to help. Someone had called the sheriff, but he got there too late. I crawled to Molly, she was unconscious, but breathing, still breathing." Momma put her head in her hands and sobbed into them, so Honey continued the story.

Honey

"The men carried Molly to her parent's house. They called Natalie and the Doctor from Corbin came too. She had a lot of damage to her face, mostly. He had broken her nose and the bones around her eye, her front teeth were missing. She had several broken ribs and some broken fingers, probably caused from trying to protect herself. They did everything they could to help her, but then she miscarried and they just couldn't get the bleeding to stop. She was just too weak. We sat with her in the last moments, as she knew that her life was about to be over. She squeezed Sarah's hand and whispered, 'I love you,' to her parents and then closed her eyes and peacefully fell asleep." Honey paused a long time trying to compose herself.

"He damaged her so much, they weren't going to be able to open her casket. Her parents had her cremated and left to go back to New York soon after her wake. Though the sheriff tried to find Colton for a little while, he never did. Colton had taken off into the mountain, and no one knew the land better than he did. Rumor was, he went high up on Pine Mountain and built him a little cabin and lived there, coming into town only to steal what he couldn't find on the land. After a while, some men went to live close by and they formed a gang, a commune of sorts, and did whatever they wanted, no one could stop them because no one knew the mountain like they did. I heard they all died in a robbery gone wrong many years ago, but not before they caused a lot of people lots of pain. The locals talk about seeing their ghosts and hearing their shouts on long nights. I hope it's the shouts of the damned in Hell they hear."

She shook her head and we sat there in silence as I grieved for a young woman I had never met.

CHAPTER SIXTEEN:

That weekend, Jayce was coming to stay with Momma and Honey went to stay with her daughter in Louisville, we both needed a break and Momma needed a fresh face for a few days. As I drove home, I felt some guilt that Kevin and I kissed, but it only happened the one time and neither of us had brought it up, since. I reasoned it was just kisses for old time's sake. I wondered how it would be to see Steve after a month of phone calls only. We talked only in brief conversations on the phone: his work, Momma's health, the baseball game on TV, his basketball league, his softball league, and ended with a good night. I hoped that maybe absence made the heart grow fonder for him and fantasized that there would be flowers waiting for me, champagne in a bucket, rose petals on the bed, and soft music playing on the stereo. He would meet me at the door and sweep me into a long hug, then slow dance me down the hall, and

260

between kisses he would tell me how much he had missed me, it would be the whole works. When we made it to the bedroom, the bed would be neatly made with the covers invitingly open, candles glowing all around the room and rose petals spread on the bed. He would slowly kiss me and undress me and we would make long and tender love. When I pulled up in the driveway on Friday night. I grabbed my bag and ran in the door laughingly shouting, "Honey, I'm home!!"

He wasn't home. My house looked like a pig sty, dishes piled into the sink, the trash can overflowed with paper plates, the table next to his recliner covered in glasses and dishes and a spilled salt shaker. Nasty bits of stuff stuck to my shoes as I walked through the house. I don't even want to describe what the bathroom looked like. What a disaster!

I must have stood there for several minutes with my mouth open in shock. OK, I never really thought there would be flowers and romance, but I didn't expect this end of the spectrum either. As I stood in the foyer, gaping at the mess, Steve pulled into the driveway, then walked in the front door. "Hey! I didn't expect you this early," he said, making no move to hug me or kiss me.

"Yeah, I uh, Jayce came early and I wanted to get here before dark, so I just came on. I was going to surprise you. Ummm, didn't the cleaning lady come?" I tried to act casual so he wouldn't accuse me of picking a fight, always the peace keeper.

"Yeah, we gotta talk about that! You know I hate people going through my stuff, I told her not to come back and got my money back from her, you paid her way too much. What were you thinking?" he grumbled, obviously not worried about causing a fight. "It's just housework, a few minutes of your time and it will be great."

"I can't do this is in a few minutes, Steve, it's disgusting."

"Well, what do you expect me to do? I work a full time job, this is your job. You ain't working this summer."

I sighed and counted to ten in my mind.

But, he just couldn't stop there, he never did understand my sighs and facial expressions, "So what's for supper? I'm starving!"

"I just got here. Why don't we go out tonight and I can get things in order tomorrow?"

"No. I'm not in the mood to eat out. You can just whip something up, I don't care what it is. You might want to run to the grocery though, we're out of everything. I thought you would stop on your way in."

"No. How could I get groceries if I didn't know what we needed?"

"Well, don't worry about it then. I will grab a snack for now and you can get to the grocery store. I'm going to play basketball tonight anyway at the middle school. They had an opening and our league took it while we could. I won't be home until about 9:00, so that should give you plenty of time to shop and cook. Then, we can make up for lost time!" He winked at me and patted my butt, I about vomited. Really? He thought I wanted to 'make up for lost time' with

263

the man who greeted me with filth and demands? Surely after 25 years of marriage, he knew better!

He went into the bedroom to change into his basketball clothes calling back, "This guy at work today…"

I went into immediate shut down mode, uttering "Uh huh, yes, really?" at all the right moments as he went through a long story of the gossip I had missed at his workplace; even though that's what we had talked about on the telephone every night.

"So, Steve," I interrupted, "do you have other plans for this weekend?"

"Well, yeah. I volunteered to umpire kids' ball games tomorrow, the other umps they have don't know what they're doing, so I told them I'd just do it. I have to be there at 8:00. I want to be there in time to work with their pitchers and catchers, none of the coaches are teaching those kids right. It should be over by 5:00 or so. I'll be home around then to eat with you. Then, tomorrow night is poker night at Hank's. Sunday, I am open until about 5, then it's regular basketball league night. Man, I'm going to be tired for work on Monday. 4:30 comes awful early in the morning you know!" He chuckled at the same joke he had been telling since he started this job twenty-three years ago.

"So, let me get this straight. I haven't been home for almost a month, we've seen each other twice since the end of May, and the one weekend I manage to come in, planning it around your work schedule, you make plans to be gone all weekend?" I could hear my voice rising and becoming shrill like it does when I am upset.

"You know that I play ball on Sundays and they needed me to help tomorrow. Besides, I need this me time. I can't take care of you and Emily if I don't take care of myself first you know. You've had a whole month off, I need a break too." He replied with heat.

Speechless, I thought, "When did he think he took care of us? Emily lived in New York and told me last night they hadn't talked in over two weeks, he never returned her calls, so she quit calling. And, did he think taking care of my dying mother was a 'break'?"

He dropped a kiss on my forehead, "I will see you sometime around 9:30. I can't wait for some of your good cooking," then he smacked my butt, again, as he walked out the door, got into his truck and left.

I looked at the clock, it was 6:45. He had been home exactly fifteen minutes before leaving. Tearing up, I walked into the kitchen and emptied the dishes out of the dishwasher. After seeing the crud on the dishes on the counter, I emptied the sink and cleaned it, then began pouring the water in with dish soap in order to wash them before filling the dishwasher. I watched the suds and water filling the sink, planning in my head what I would cook that night, what I needed at the grocery and what I would clean next. As I planned, I felt that same cloud of hopelessness envelop me that I lived with since Christian passed away. I knew that the rest of my life consisted of pushing my own needs and desires to the background to take care of everyone else. For many years, I stayed in my marriage because I knew Christian and Emily needed a solid home front, then I couldn't upset Emily, she needed a family as intact as I could make it.

It didn't matter that I constantly felt Steve's giant thumb pushing down on me, taking from me, always taking and never giving back what I needed. Was it too much to ask that he treasure me? Was it too much to ask that he act as a partner to me? I mean, really, the man couldn't even walk beside me, he always walked two steps ahead of me! He controlled me in so many ways, and I allowed him to. It was easier to bow down to him and just do what he wanted. It's what I did. This summer, though, acted as an eye opener. I wanted what my parents lived, I wanted a love that surpassed time and understanding. This wasn't it. Steve didn't love me, he used me. He used me as a housekeeper, a cook, a sex object. He did not like me to use my brain or offer an opinion that differed from his. If I didn't fully agree with him, he accused me of 'not supporting' him. The more I thought about how life would be living with him, the angrier I became. So what, if I lived alone the rest of my life. At least I could take care of me. I could support myself, I didn't need him. "Fuck you," I whispered the terrible F word. It felt so good I said it again, louder this time, "Fuck you!" Then louder until I shouted it over and over at the time of my voice. I felt liberated and strong when I stopped and the house settled quietly around me again.

"I don't have to take this!" I said to the silent house, then I shouted as loud as I could, "I don't have to do this anymore. There is more to me than this." I turned off the faucet and away from the steaming water in the sink, went to my bedroom and put more clothes in another suitcase. I then put the cases back in the trunk of my car, came back, got my purse and locked the door. I left.

I left. I can't believe I just left. For once, I didn't just pout and do what I was expected to do. I left. For a while, I drove aimlessly around town. I stopped at the little mall and walked around the shops, not really interested in anything I saw, I just didn't know what to do with myself. I knew I wasn't going to return home to that mess. It was a perfect metaphor for my marriage I decided. He messed it, I tended it. He left, I stayed. I cared, he didn't. It was time to get out, if I wanted anything left of myself.

Suddenly, I felt lighter than I had in years, a bounce entered my step as I walked past store after store. I stopped at Starbuck's and bought a cup of the coffee he deemed way too expensive to buy, then, sat down at a little bistro table and considered my options. I was off for an entire weekend. I could go back to Momma's, but we both needed the break from each other, we were getting on each other's nerves. I could go back to the house – that wasn't an option. I could stay with a friend, but I didn't want to intrude. Finally, I called the Holiday Inn and reserved a room for the weekend. I could swim, use the fitness and business centers as needed and make plans from there.

As I sat there planning, an older gentleman walked over, "May I sit with you?"

"Of course," I answered, absently, thinking there must not be any chairs available. I looked up and realized all the other chairs sat empty and he smiled at me.

He said, "I know this is probably inappropriate, but I think you are so pretty, and I would love to take you out to dinner tonight, or for drinks, your pick."

I gaped at him and then laughed, "I can't. I'm married, but you have truly made my day."

He sighed then rose and handed me a business card with his name and number, "Here's my number if you ever change your mind. I think you have the most amazing hazel eyes."

I took the card and said good-bye. I realized it had been a long time since a stranger had looked at me as being pretty. It felt good. Good things were happening today, I decided.

I went to the room I reserved and as I entered into the quiet coolness, my phone rang, it was

Steve's number. I hesitated and then hit the silence button. I wasn't ready, or strong enough, to deal with him at this point. When the tone sounded indicating a message, I played it, "Uh Van? You didn't leave a note. Are you at the grocery still? Did you make me something to eat? I'm starving."

I turned my phone onto silent, took off my clothes and laid in the bed. All the interrupted nights with Momma made me so tired, that I fell sound asleep within moments and slept until 8:30 the next morning. I got up and made my way downstairs for the free breakfast, then checked my phone when I returned to the room. It showed six calls and two more messages from Steve, "I called your mom's house, they don't know where you are. This is stupid. Let me know where you are." I knew he would be on the baseball field and not answer his telephone, so I took the coward's way out and left a message.

"Steve, I am fine. I am not coming back to the house. You obviously don't want me or need me, so I am going to make other arrangements. I will call you next week." After twenty-five years of marriage, I could sum our relationship up in a few words, we neither wanted nor needed each other.

I didn't quite know what to do with myself after that. I couldn't go back to that house, I would cave in and do whatever Steve wanted. I wanted to be sure to stay strong and true to me and to my purpose. Suddenly, I had a great idea! I was here in Lexington with a hotel room at my disposal. I would call Kevin to come and join me. We had been flirting around for a while, so why not? I went upstairs to make a list of the things I would need to make the night romantic, and then, already excited, I called Kevin. "Hey!" I said when he answered.

"Hey back! What are you doing? I thought you went home," he answered.

"Well, I did. Things changed." I told him about what I found at home. "I have a proposal to make to you," I purred into the phone.

"I'm listening," he said with a smile in his voice.

"I have this hotel room all to my lonely self. Why don't you come up and stay with me tonight and tomorrow?" I held my breath, but expected to hear he was on the way. However, I heard a long pause instead.

"Ummm, Kevin, are you still there?" I questioned with a hollow feeling in my stomach.

"Lavani, you don't know how much I want to come up there and be with you. I can't believe I'm saying this…"

"You aren't coming? It's fine. No big deal. Don't worry about it," I guessed I had been misreading him all along. My face burned with embarrassment.

"It's not like that. Please don't think that. I just don't want to do anything you are going to regret. I don't want to be the one you turn to when you are hurt and angry. If we are together, I want it to be because that's what we chose, not out of anger. I don't want any chance that you regret this," he tried to explain.

Honestly, I could barely hear him. The blood roared in my head. I needed to get off the phone before he heard me cry, "Sure," I agreed, "I understand. Uh, listen, my phone is beeping, Emily is on the other line (I lied) I have to go," and I hung up before even saying good bye.

I laid my phone on the table and put my face in both hands, scrubbing away the tears and. What the heck is wrong with me, I wondered. Is it my weight? My appearance? Why does no one want me? I knew, deep inside, Kevin was probably right, but I didn't want to deal with it.

Finally, I got up and filled the tub with bubbles and hot water and soaked until my fingers and toes wrinkled. I read in the tub until the water turned cold and then got out and dressed in my pajamas even though it was early afternoon. I checked my phone and both Steve and Kevin had called, but I didn't return either one. I couldn't handle it. I drew the curtains against the sun, then turned off all the lights, except for the one by the bed and opened Momma's journals again and fell back into her life. I spent that day and the next sleeping and reading.

CHAPTER SEVENTEEN:

Sarah

After Molly's memorial service, Sarah finished her senior year. She applied and was accepted at Berea College, went through the motions of school, skipped her prom and her senior trip and graduated with a perfect grade point average. Honey and Leonard pointed out that, although her grade point average was perfect, she was not selected to be either Valedictorian or Salutatorian, neither did she receive any of the local scholarships, they were angry. She just shook her head and remained silent, what good did it do to fight? Besides, what did it matter? Every day, she missed Molly. Rumors circulated for several weeks about her death, but she never had mattered much and everything died down in the excitement of ballgames and dances and prom. Sarah just went to her classes, silently, and did her work and finished what she needed to finish. She skipped graduation day, she didn't want to go through the ceremony with people she never liked who never liked her either. On that day, she went into the woods surrounding the farm and found a large rock and lay there in the sun until Honey found her and just laid beside her silently until they got up and went to the house to cook dinner.

Honey had married Leonard by this time, and Sarah liked him very much. He wasn't much to look at, but he helped the kids with their homework every night, and cracked jokes until everyone smiled and laughed. The house that had held such silent sorrow since the death of her mother rang with laughter. Sarah was grateful to him. She and the kids would have just given Honey and him the farm and house, but he had insisted he pay for it, otherwise it would never be his. They went to the bank and had the place surveyed, then negotiated a fair price. He put the money into seven bank accounts split equally every month. It would be more than enough to see her through her college career. Her brothers would not have to work as much on weekends and summer and it lightened the load for everyone. He began raising tobacco and wheat and other money crops and hired the boys to help him. They insisted he only pay them half the going wage because they were living in the house and wanted to contribute. He also paid the girls a similar allowance to clean and work the gardens and take care of the home place and Honey quit working for others. All of them were much happier, it was a better way of life for them all, and Sarah felt relieved that she could go to college in the summer and not put a burden on anyone.

Once she had been accepted into Berea College, she tested out of all the required classes, but in talking to her advisor had learned she could come that summer to work and take a couple of classes to prepare to start her degree program. They assigned her to cafeteria service, which she didn't mind, it was a job after all, and she took a math course and an English course. Once she entered college life, she found out that

278

most people didn't care about her heritage there, they accepted all people, and she made friends quickly and easily. She enjoyed her time there and worked hard. Every night she wrote a letter to Callaway and every day she checked her CPO for letters back, sometimes she wouldn't get any for days, then there would be six or seven in her box waiting for her. She would carefully arrange them by the date and then savor them in her room. They wrote of the things people in love write: school, friendships, missing each other, every day events. Callaway never wrote much about the war, just some funny stories about his fellow soldiers and their antics, but Sarah sensed a heartbreak underneath some of his passages that he would never come out and say. There was, however, one letter that really touched her.

My Dearest Sarah,

I love you. There, I've already said it, so you don't have to look at the bottom of my letter to know it. I'm glad you are liking Berea so well, and really glad the people there aren't stupid and racist. You are finally getting your chance to really shine and I hope you shine like the star you are. But, in all that shining, I hope you don't forget that I'm standing under the sky wishing for you. I can't wait until we can marry and make our own way in life.

It's been a hard day. The rain has lasted all day long and the very air feels and smells like I'm breathing in sweat. My clothes are soaked clear through, heck, I think my skin is soaked all the way through. I'd like to have a couple of days just baking on the farm hoeing my garden or setting tobacco. I know that the plant beds have been set back home and I heard Mom and Joe have seeded a lettuce bed too. I bet she makes it the way I like it, with radishes and hot bacon grease, she does some magic thing with vinegar and sugar in there and it's the best eating of spring time. I guess home is just on my mind more and more these days as I get closer to the end of my tour.

You remember Emmit? The funny guy from Tennessee? We've been in the same unit since we enlisted. He got shot today. Right in the head. He fell in front of me and there wasn't even time to say good-bye, he was gone that fast. I grabbed his body and my buddies and I got out. Now, he's on his way home. I wrote a letter to his mom. I just told her what a great guy he was and how he made us laugh all the time. I told her he was a good man – a good friend. I don't know if it helps her, I don't think much could help a momma who lost her child. Damn this war. Damn this war. Damn this war. I wonder sometimes, why we are even here fighting it. I wonder why I just keep dodging bullets and don't let one hit me so I can come home too. But, I won't. I love you, and you love me, so we owe it to each other to take care of ourselves, until we can take care of each other.

I hope you don't mind that all I want to do is farm. You know how I like the land. I want to raise my own food and my own animals, though, after all this, I'm not so sure I could hunt again. I think I've seen enough death for now.

I've been reading about Honeybees. Did you know there is only one female boss in a hive? She's the queen, and the only one who has babies, and is the only one that the other bees listen to. I think you are the queen in my hive. Though, knowing us, we won't always be listening to the other.

I love you. I miss you. I can't wait for the day I can hold you in my arms. I can't wait to see you on our wedding day. I promise to always cherish you and work hard for you. I promise that you will be the only queen I will ever honor.

Love,

Callaway

Sarah held the letter close to her heart, then laid it on the bed as she gathered up her books and notebooks. She hadn't heard from Callaway in over two weeks, and she was starting to get very worried. His letters never spaced out this far. On impulse, she put the letter into her notebook and then walked out of the dorm room and down the hall. Today, she planned to attend her last general education class, a religion class. Tomorrow morning, she would head out bright and early for the last clinical rotation of her nursing class. The four years she spent here flew by! She waved at some friends, but didn't hurry to catch up, she enjoyed the spring air and the walk. As she walked, she continued to plan out the next phase of her life. Next week was finals week, then she would begin studying for the Nursing Exam. After that, she would work in a local hospital while attending classes at the Midwifery School. She had applied and been accepted, assuming she passed the exam. Her dreams were finally coming true. No other child would lose their mother because of racist doctors, she determined. Natalie offered her an internship at home with her, but Sarah thought about just going somewhere and being a stranger. It would be easier to make new friends and help other women, than try to climb the wall of racism and help the women who used to be her classmates.

Lavani

I enjoyed Momma's entries about her time at Berea College. She talked about it while we grew up, but I never realized how much she treasured the acceptance she found there. I knew the campus was beautiful, but I never before understood the spirit of the place was beautiful as well. This school helped poor Appalachians achieve their dreams, instead of turning them away into their poverty and need. The professors taught them to serve others, to make this world a better place, and they lived their teaching. Momma never wrote that she felt judged or discriminated against, in fact, it was quite the opposite. She wrote about the parties she attended, Mountain and Labor Day activities, the street dances, the friends she hung out with. She wrote about fun and good times, and her voice in the journals sounded much stronger and more like the woman I knew? Was it this place that helped my momma become the strong and confident woman I knew? If, indeed, it was, then I would forever be grateful to Natalie for introducing Momma to the college and to the college for accepting her.

For the first time since I started reading her journals, Momma fit in. She found out she could make lots of friends and no one cared her mother came from Native American stock. Momma began to bloom while in Berea College; she learned to love herself and she began to help others bloom. Her journals shared the amazing growth in four years that my momma experienced.

I turned back to her journal from her senior year.

Sarah

Sarah's thought process preoccupied her mind so much she didn't pay attention to the large presence behind her. He stepped out of the shadows behind the dorm when she exited and stayed a couple of paces behind, just observing her movements. Suddenly, he acted, he ran forward a couple of steps and grabbed her around the waist, twirling her around and around until she was dizzy, laughing in her ears.

"Callaway!" she shrieked, and twisting in his arms put her mouth right on his and kissed him in front of everyone, "Callaway, Callaway," she said between kisses. He finally let her down and she heard the applause from the other students passing by. She blushed, but didn't care, "When did you get here? I was so worried! Why didn't you tell me? How…"

"Sarah, I sent you all that weeks ago. I bet you just didn't get my letters."

She looked at him standing so handsome and tall in his uniform. "I don't want to leave you, but I have to get to class. I can't miss because we are studying for finals."

"Think it'll be ok if I just join you?" he asked

"Well, we can always ask!"

Callaway sat through that class with Sarah. She didn't hear a word the professor spoke, she sat and drank him in with her eyes. His face looked the same, though tired. His tan skin glowed against the olive of his uniform and his blue eyes looked a little harder, more alert that before. He watched the people around him and seemed to be aware of every movement in the room, even the casual shifting of position in the chairs caught his attention. She wondered about the things he had seen that created this sense of ultra-awareness, but knew he wouldn't tell her until he was ready.

He walked her back to the dorm later, and they sat and talked in the lobby until late that night. He told her a little about the war, mostly funny stories of his comrades in the barracks and the towns, and about how much he missed her. He told her about the money he saved to buy a farm. They talked about where they wanted to live and what they wanted to do.

"I figure we'll get married as soon as you graduate. I hope you don't mind living with nothin' but a farmer. It's all I ever wanted to be," he said after a long time of chatting and kissing. "That way we can go on and get us a place to live. You'll want to be near a hospital or something, so it'll have to be close to town, I reckon."

"What? I can't get married this summer, I was accepted to the Frontier School of Midwifery and I'm starting school in August. I have to live in Hyden and finish my training. Then we have to live somewhere rural so that I can help the women. I don't want to live near the city!"

He looked at her quietly, "I thought we planned to get married when you graduated."

"But, Callaway, you knew that my dream is to become a midwife."

"I wouldn't stand in the way of your dream, but I thought I was included in it."

"You are! You are part of my dream, I just can't marry you yet. I have to finish my training, first, and …" She tried to explain.

Callaway stood, "I have to go tonight and find a room, anyway. I need to ponder on this for a while. I'll see you tomorrow. I love you." He bent over and kissed Sarah, nodded to her whispered I love you too and walked out.

Sarah was stunned. They spent so much time talking about their dreams, his to be a farmer, hers to be a nurse midwife, that she never realized he didn't understand she would need more training after college. She got up and walked up to her room, her joy at seeing Callaway tempered with the worry of upsetting him.

Truth and Grace

CHAPTER EIGHTEEN:

The next day, Callaway was waiting for her when she went out the front door. He walked beside her holding her hand as they headed to the nursing building so she could catch a ride to the hospital where she was finishing her clinicals. "I thought it through last night. You need to go on and do the training. I ain't goin' anywhere. I'm gonna find us a farm and get things ready to bring you back there as my bride. You just remember who you are gonna marry, and we'll be alright."

"You are a good man," Sarah whispered with tears in her eyes. The rest of the weekend he stayed there, they spent touring campus and hanging out with her friends. He was always willing to drive them anywhere and they spent some time in Richmond and Lexington exploring. Wherever Sarah went, Callaway also went. On Sunday evening, though, he had to leave.

"I'm going home to see Mom, she doesn't even know I'm stateside," he told Sarah. I'm going to stay there for a time while I find us that perfect place." He hesitated, "I'm gonna try to find Colton while I'm there. I just wanted you to know. We haven't talked about Molly, but I'm so sorry Sarah. I really loved her and I can't believe what Colton did. I need to talk to him."

Sarah looked away as tears filled her eyes, "Callaway, I know he's your brother, but there's something evil in him. Please, please don't try to contact him. I'm afraid he'll hurt you."

"He won't hurt me. Sarah, do you believe things come down to us through the blood?" He was pacing and nervous.

Puzzled she replied, "Some things do, I think. Why?"

"I need to tell you about something I ain't never told nobody."

Lavani

Momma explained at the beginning of the next entry that she wrote the next part of her journal in the words my father told her. She explained that she wanted to keep his story in his words because it was his story and she didn't want to change it. I figured if she didn't have every word right, she at least had the gist of it. The teardrops she shed as she wrote, still encircled some of the words, mine joined them.

It was hard for me to read what he said, but I knew it would help me understand him better and, ultimately, my momma better. Wasn't that the point of reading her journals? She shared her story with me, so I could understand my story better.

I shifted to get a bit more comfortable and thought about getting a glass of water. A thought soon lost in the reading of Daddy's words.

Callaway

"This evil you see in Colton? It's the same evil that was in my dad. I know I never told you, I was too embarrassed, but my dad used to beat on me and Colton and my mom – a lot. When we were little, he'd take us to the woods and get a switch off of a tree and make us pull down our pants and he'd whale away until we bled from the cuts that little switch made. If Mom tried to interfere, he'd start punching her. He was 'beating the devil' out of us, he'd say. As we grew older, he got worse and worse...

We were just twelve years old and our dad had been drinking steady for two days. He did this every now and then. Sober he was bad, but drunk he was brutal. Our mom tried to keep us out of the house as much as possible, sending us on errands or out into the back fields to do work, but we had to come back to the house for supper and sleep. Thankfully, tomorrow was Monday and we would be at school. We quietly eased into the house to see our mother at the stove stirring something, when she turned around her lip was split and she had a black eye. Putting her finger on her mouth to tell us to be quiet, she started setting the table. I don't know how Colton felt, I assumed it was the same way I did, I was boiling mad, but still scared of Father.

We went into the small room where the water was already waiting for us and washed our hands and faces carefully and silently. One word, one speck of dirt could set him off. Still silently, we made our way back to the table. He sat there, at the head of the table, glowering at us, 'took you boys long enough," then he bowed his head and prayed a long disjointed prayer about sin and evil. Finally, after he said, "amen," we started to pass around the dishes.

There was no conversation, in fact when Father cleared his throat we all jumped, 'Pass the beans,' he said to Colton. Colton reached for the beans and knocked over his glass of milk. It was all Father needed. He jumped up already reaching to release the buckle on his belt, 'Boy! How many times have I told you to be careful? How many times have I told you not to waste? I work hard for that milk you carelessly spilled, hard!' He grabbed Colton's arm and pulled him away from the table, hitting him fast and hard with the belt and the buckle, spit flew from his mouth as he shouted and just kept hitting. Colton screamed and pulled and tried to free himself, but it only made Father angrier, he held tighter and beat harder.

Finally, I couldn't stand it, I pushed my way between them, "Stop it Father, you'll kill him!"

"Then you'll take his beating!" and he started in on me. Oh it hurt. The stings of the leather were nothing compared to the pain of the buckle, but I just covered his face and took the strokes until Father was too tired to hit more. I didn't want him to go back and beat Colton or my mom anymore. When he stopped, Colton and me both lay on the floor, bleeding and whimpering. Momma must have tried to interfere at some point, because when Father went slamming out of the house hollering about useless pussy boys, I looked over and saw her sitting against the wall, with a large cut on her forehead where the belt buckle had bit on a backswing and her nose bled.

Gingerly, I got up, "Mom, are you ok?"

Colton got up too and looked me straight in the eyes, "Don't you ever step between us again and take my beating. I'm going to kill the Son of a Bitch for doing this to us."

'Colton, don't talk like that,' Mom said, "you aren't like him. Neither of you are.'

'You know, Mom, maybe I am evil like he's always sayin', but I ain't takin another beatin'.' With that, he walked up the stairs to the bedroom we shared. I stayed downstairs to help Mom do the dishes and other night time chores.

Mom, let's go. Let's just leave outta here and go away where he can never find us, I begged her.

'I can't Sweetie. Don't you think I've thought of that a million times? I ain't got no money, he sees to it that if we need to spend something, he buys it. I can't take off without money.'

Then let's go to Gram's and Pepaw's.

'No, I tried that a long time ago. You know how religious they are. Dad just brought me back here and put me out on the porch, 'You are married. You promised to cleave unto one another no matter what. You're his and I ain't putting asunder what God has joined together. I'm stuck Callaway, there ain't nowhere for me to be. When you boys get older, though, I want you to go. I love you, but when you get your education, you go. Don't be a man like that. I'm afraid Colton is too much like your father, but you have something different inside of you.
300

Maybe you have a little of me. There's a gentleness to your spirit, a willingness to help and accept others. Don't you think I've heard about the little redskin family you've taken care of all these years? That's proof, there's a heart inside of you. Now, get to bed, you have school tomorrow, I'll finish up here.'

I kissed her then headed up to bed, trying to figure out what we could do to get away from Father. Colton was lying there, fully clothed. 'Callway, I'm gonna kill him. I want you to know that.'

No, Colton, please don't. It's still a sin. Let's just figure out how to get Mom and us out of this town and away from him. We spent some time trying to figure out a plan. For weeks we argued and talked and worked to figure it out. But, never did come up with anything feasible."

He paused here, in his story and just looked at his beautiful Sarah. She listened to him, leaned towards him with compassion in her eyes. He hoped the next part of his story wouldn't change the way she saw him.

"About two months later, Father went to chop some wood back on the ridge of the farm. Colton played hooky that day, He claimed the last pretty day of fall demanded him to, and he just needed out before the snows came. He did this frequently, so I never thought anything about it. I just waved at him and watched him slip into the woods on the side of the road. When we met up after school, I noticed Colton's hand looked a bit bruised and his jacket had new a tear on the sleeve. "Now who you been fighting? You know Mom don't like us to fight."

Colton just grinned at me, a fierce grin, 'oh I met a feller by the railroad tracks and we got to fooling around is all. He slung his arm around me, 'Brother, things is about to get a whole lot better. I got me a feelin'!'

That night, Father didn't come home. Early the next morning, Mom woke us. 'I'm worried about your father. I've called some men and they are going looking for him. Do you want to go with them?' she questioned us, nervously. I think, even before we went she sensed what we might find. As a good mother, she wanted to protect   us.

We got up and pulled on their clothes, since we were the ones who knew the farm the best, the men let us lead the way to the ridge where Father had said he'd be chopping. In the rising dawn of the morning, we found him, what was left of him, face down in a pool of his own blood. The sheriff said it looked like maybe someone had come up behind him and hit him in the back of the head with a big stick, knocking him down and weakening him. Then he'd been beaten pretty badly. His face was bruised and his nose was broken. Finally, whoever did it had taken the ax Father was using and buried it in his throat. Animals had gotten at the body during the night, so there was a lot of damage. I have to admit, I puked in the bushes. I looked over to see if Colton was sick too, but he was standing there looking at that body and wearing a little smile.

They never did find out who killed Father. Truth be told, no one really cared. He cheated and blustered his way through his job at the coal mine then fought his way through the town. Everyone liked Mom and us boys were popular in school and though no one had said anything about it, I guess they noticed the bruises and soreness of all of us.

The sheriff figured that someone from the card game the night before had gotten to him." Here, Callaway paused for a long time, "But, I knew. We never discussed it, Colton changed after that. He became harder, more willing to fight and he spent more time out in the mountain. I knew Mom worried about him, so did I, but there was no reachin' him.

Colton's prediction came true, life did get better. The life insurance and social security kept us on our feet financially until Mom met Joe at church. He's a good man, he took us under his wing and we liked him fine. They sold our farm and moved onto his and he taught us how to hunt and forage and gather. He became the father we needed.

But, sometimes, in the stillness of the night, I lay awake and wonder. I wonder what kind of kid could kill his father and not be sorry. I watched Colton with new eyes and knew that he harbored that same cruelty our father possessed. I saw it when he broke someone's bone on the football field, or even when he killed a deer and dressed it, there was a delight in the causing of pain and misery, rather than the thankfulness and reverence I felt."

At this point, Callaway looked straight into Sarah's trusting eyes, "What worries me the most though, was that I knew what Colton had done, knew it with all my heart; yet, I said nothing to no one about it. In fact, I was grateful because Father was gone from our lives. There were no more beatings, no more yelling and our Mom was happy. What kind of person does it make me that I'm glad Colton killed Father?"

Lavani

Momma's journal didn't detail her response, but I imagined she must have done what any woman would, she hugged him and reassured him that it was understandable he felt relieved that the beatings and cruelty had stopped. I closed the journal. My wonderful, amazing and tender Daddy had been savagely beaten? I couldn't believe a parent could ever hurt a child like that. It made sense, now, why Momma had always been the disciplinarian in our home. Whenever Daddy was angry, he would fold his lips together and walk outside for a little while. I realized, it was in order to keep his own demons at bay.

It made me wonder how this made his mother, my sweet MawMaw feel when she stopped to think about it. I'm sure she had to suspect that one son had murdered his own father, she knew he had murdered Molly. She had to wonder if there had been others. If she, herself, had ever been on that list, or his twin, or her new husband. She had to fear that he would come visit her. Then what? She would be desperately happy to see this child of hers, but would she have to call the police to turn him in? Would they put him in prison where her outdoor loving son would wilt away? No matter what he was – fugitive, abuser, liar, murderer – he was still hers. She had still held him as a baby and prayed over him and dreamed over him. She had sacrificed her body and face many times so that he wouldn't get beaten, and would do so without thinking again.

To me, I think this existence would be almost worse than the death of a child. She could never see him again, she would always worry about him as he lived life on the run. She would hear rumors about his cruelty and his legendary temper, she would see police or the federals climb the mountain and worry that this time, this time, they would find her son and either drag him down to his death, or kill him there. She knew what he deserved and what her neighbors said, and that poor little girl's family that must be devastated, but he was still her son. She couldn't have been ready to lose him.

I lost my son. Actually, that sentence really tends to piss me off. I did NOT lose my son. I was not that irresponsible of a parent. I knew exactly where he was. He was in the ICU at UK Hospital awaiting the transplant that never came

307

when his body simply gave out. He did NOT lose his fight to cystic fibrosis. He was never a loser. He battled hard and long and with more grace and dignity and humor than a person two or three times his age would. He made sure to tell people he loved them and designed his own funeral service. He was secure in his faith and not afraid to die, only afraid to leave us.

I did not lose my son; but, I lost so much. His humor and wit, his love and strength. My first born, my boy, my sportsman, my aspiring dreams and hopes, my prom goer, my graduate, my college student, my daughter in law and my grandchildren. I lost a lot, but I did not lose him.

After all this time, I still felt so angry, at God at people, at the world - angry at c fucking f – enraged at fate, karma, kismet, THE PLAN whatever it was, that forced him away from us. I'm angry at every single person whose loved one died and they chose to bury the organs with the body. I thought, "They are just as responsible for his death as the damn disease. I try to have compassion, I try to understand their grief, but they killed my son. They are killers."

I knew CODA members would probably be open mouthed in shock and anger, but I can't help how I felt. I've imagined the trio of letters I could write so many times I feel like I've printed them in every paper in the United States. All of them went something like this:

> *Dear Grieving Parents,*
>
> *You are killers. You had the way of saving my child and, letting eight   other people live with their family and friends. You possessed the one way to cure so many diseases. But, you chose to be selfish and short sighted. You chose spite and despair. My child would be alive now if you made the right choice. Because of you, he is as dead as if you held a gun to his head and pulled the trigger. You wouldn't listen, didn't care, wanted not to deal with it. You are murderers and you murdered my child. My beautiful child, who asked to leave his own organs, even as they failed him.*

I hate you. I am in your grieving club because of you. I hate you.

Sincerely

,

A Grieving Mother

Dear Kismet or Karma,

You suck!

Dear God,

Why?

Maybe I should have actually sent them to the newspapers. Maybe it was time that one person spoke up and said the truth. The truth we all must think, the truth that doctors and nurses know, if organs are not donated, people die. Children die. Hopes, dreams, thoughts, – it all dies but the love and the pain. But, of course, I never sent the letter. I tucked it deep into the broken pieces of my heart and faked compassion or walked away when parents told me, "I just couldn't think about them

310

hurting his body after he died, " or, "It was just too much to deal with at the time," or my personal favorite, "He came into this world with those organs, he should go out with them." People are stupid, and I'm a coward.

Truth and Grace

CHAPTER NINETEEN:

Sarah

It was their wedding day. Sarah felt so nervous and excited that she simply couldn't sit still. She paced a little bit, smoothed down the lacy mini skirt wedding dress she and Honey had found on a wild trip into Lexington. It didn't look like a traditional dress with it's short length, above her knees. But she loved the long lace sleeves and tiny buttons in the back. She fooled with the birdcage veil over her ear and waited, impatiently to see Callaway's truck pull into the lane.

Callaway would be there in just a few minutes to pick her up so they could go to the Justice of the Peace and say their vows. Honey and Leonard were hosting a party this weekend to celebrate, but there hadn't been time to plan a wedding. Sarah laughed, knowing that rumors would spread in this small town they had chosen and that people would be counting the months until the arrival of a baby; but, there was no baby, it was just time to become Callaway's wife.

She was the one who put it off. She took the time to go to the Frontier School of Nurse Midwifery, Callaway would have married right after her college graduation, but she wanted to wait. She went to Hyden and learned all she had ever dreamed of knowing and then began to put her knowledge into practice working with different midwives in several counties to learn how to be integrated into a community and how to keep women and babies safe and healthy. Before she knew it, a year had passed as she worked hard. Now, it was time to be a woman and to marry her man.

It almost didn't happen. After her college graduation, she and Callaway had picked this community to live in. He took the money from his time in the army and bought a farm. For now, he was living in the one bedroom cabin that was on it when he bought it, but they had been making house plans for several months. Callaway had used the time while she was away to plow the land and plant the crops that they would need, not just for survival, but also what they would need to prosper. He was a good worker, but always aware of the beauty and the needs of the land. She could envision their farm as a series of half circles. In the middle, smallest circle would be where they would build their house and garage. It would have a yard and pretty flowers in the beds. Around that, in a larger half circle, he planted a huge fruit and vegetable garden, and a small herb garden for her medicines and cooking use. Between the two gardens, he constructed a small shed that held the tools needed for those areas: hoes and rakes, trowels and spikes. In the circle around the gardens, he placed a shed for his equipment and a greenhouse for the plants. Surrounding each of these were large yards that held the chicken coop and turkey yard. He let the chicken and turkeys freely roam through the gardens, saying they were a free way to take care of the pests and fertilize the rest. A large barn in the same ring of space housed the animals he loved: milk cows, beef cows, pigs, and horses. Attached to that barn was a large pen for goats and further out was a shed and fields for sheep. The fields for the larger animals also led out from the back of the barns. Sarah loved to go out to the middle of the barns and sheds and listen to the peaceful talking of the animals as they went about their day. Behind the barns and the fields were the orchards.

Callaway had planted peach trees, apples trees, and pear trees. Next to the orchards lay a few long rows of grapes. He had also put a shed there to hold the specialized equipment needed for the jobs. His pride and joy were the large hives of bees housed close to the orchards and vineyard. He loved his bees, and said only one had ever stung him and that was, 'over a misunderstanding.' Beyond the orchards were the tobacco fields and the smaller wheat and corn fields. The tobacco barn stood in the middle dividing the two, attached to it was the threshing barn and storage. The wheat and corn were hauled to the storage areas attached to the animal barns to be convenient for winter's use. Beyond that, there was a large pond and the hay fields. Ringing all of that were the woods where he hunted wild animals and wild plants; he loved and nurtured everything about his land. It was a gorgeous farm; some of the old timers laughed at him, saying he didn't need all the sheds and barns, but Callaway felt they were convenient to the area and he would rather have a few minutes in the shade, than a long walk to the barn.

Being a farmer has never been easy. Callaway had to be a weather forecaster, a long term planter, an ecologist, a farm hand, a boss, a mechanic, a carpenter and a veterinarian every single day. He thrived in the environment. With his practices and understanding of Mother Nature, he was an environmentalist before it was cool.

Sarah knew it was time to marry this man. This man who patiently waited for her to finish school and training, who supported her in her chosen career and worked hard to make a good living. She hoped for a long and happy life with him, knowing he would always be her soul-mate. He would be the only man she would ever know or love.

He turned into the lane and she smiled and ran outside, down the porch stairs and flung herself into his arms. He gently pushed her back a little, "Wow, you look gorgeous!" he said.

"If you think this is pretty, you should see what I have for tonight," she blushed as she said it, but his lightning fast grin made it ok to be bold.

"Then, we better go now!" he almost shouted. He picked her up in his arms, swinging her around and around until she was laughing and dizzy then sat her in the truck. They laughed all the way to the courthouse.

When Callaway slipped his ring onto her finger, Sarah vowed her love and promises to him aloud. Inside, she vowed to never remove this symbol of their love.

Lavani

Of course, Momma wrote about her wedding nights, and the many passionate nights that followed. It would embarrass her if I shared, but the entries made me sigh with envy (well, once I got over thinking about my mother and father having sex). Her stories of their physical love proved that romance and gentleness did exist in marriage, along with the fun and the desperate needs felt by those in love.

I stopped to think about all the times I saw my momma and daddy kiss. They never showed shyness in that regard. If he left the house, they kissed. If she left the house, they kissed. The kisses were rarely chaste pecks on the cheeks. They were good long kisses on the lips. Momma and Daddy kissed like they meant it. I remembered walking into the kitchen and faking a gag when I saw Daddy had trapped Momma against the sink and turned her around to give her long slow kisses. Her hands, covered in soap suds, gripped the back of his shirt. When he let her go and walk away, she pretended to fuss at him for interrupting him, but when he turned away she grinned. I knew he laughed because of the shaking of his shoulders.

I thought all marriages were like that. Full of fun and kisses and mutual passion. Mine wasn't. All these years, and I couldn't remember even once making love while laughing and tickling, heck, I couldn't remember even once making love. Between Steve and me, we had sex. Not wanting to think about that, I picked up the next journal, the first one after the wedding and honeymoon.

Here, Momma's journals turned more to the mundane tasks of being a farmer's wife and midwife. She told funny and sad stories about the children she helped bring into the world. She spoke constantly about her love for her Callaway, and increasingly, about her desire to have a baby.

I found myself mostly skimming these entries. Although it shed some light upon my momma's feeling and emotions, I sensed the story lay in other parts. I promised myself I would come back and read these entries closer, later.

Sarah

Sarah received a call to help with the birth of a family high in the mountains. She approached this family once, while visiting a patient nearby, about calling her when it came time for the quite pregnant mother to give birth. Rudely, the woman told her, "My maw and the granny come for me. I don't need no new fangled ideas to have a baby." So, the call both surprised her and worried her.

She arrived to find that the woman had already struggled with labor for twenty four hours. Her husband became worried and sent after Sarah even though his mother in law and the Granny argued with him. He met her at the front of the house, "Ma'am, I'm much obliged you come here. Missus is cryin' and screamin' and she ain't never done that. Granny (the mountain woman) and Nanny (his mother in law) don't want you here, but my wife said call you so I did. I'll try to keep the other women from botherin' you, but I can't promise."

Sarah sighed, the process of birth could be hard enough without the interference this could bring. "OK, let's get to it, then." She strode into the small house to find it burning up, even though the day was a pleasant temperature, the fireplace was blazing and the cookstove was roaring. It felt like she walked into a wall of heat. She turned to the husband, "Why do you have it so hot in here?"

The mountain granny answered, "Any Dummy knows a house has to be hot for a newborn or they catch a chill and die," she snorted and spat a stream of tobacco spit into a close by spittoon. "We aint got need of no fancy schmancy pants to help us birth a baby."

Sarah ignored her for the moment and turned to the husband, "What's your name?"
"Johnny," he said.

"Johnny, if you trust me, do whatever I tell you."

"Yes , ma'am I will. My maw has said call you all along. If she trusts you, I do too."

"OK, first, open the windows and doors and get this house bearable. Labor is hard work and we need to make her comfortable. Get those fires banked down, they aren't necessary."

Sarah walked into the bedroom where her patient lay in bed. Her face was bright red and

Sarah could tell by her breathing how tired she was. What concerned her though, was that her mound of belly set too high. She labored but the baby didn't drop low enough to get into the birth canal. The bedding looked stained and dirty, and her nightgown twisted and snaked around her. When Johnny came in after following her orders she told him, "Wash your hands all the way up over the elbows, and your face and hair. Use soap and plenty of it. Then, bring me a change of sheets for the bed, a clean nightgown – a light one - and some washcloths and towels."

She walked up to the laboring woman, "I'm going to teach you how to breathe with your contractions to help a little bit with the pain, then I'm going to wash up really well and make you as comfortable as I possibly can. I know you hurt. I'm going to help you and together we will get this baby born. What's your name?"

"I'm Elizabeth."

"OK, Elizabeth, I will be right back." She walked out of the room to discover Johnny finished with his washing and finding the items she requested. She threw the basin of dirty water out and cleaned it with boiling water (at least one good thing the women had done) and then washed her own hands and arms.

She returned to the room, careful to touch nothing. "Johnny, clean out my basin and fill it with hot water and soap and bring it in here. I'm going to be washing my hands a great deal and I need for you to help me keep very clean so we don't make your wife and baby sick.

He rushed off to do what she asked. Sarah turned to Elizabeth's mother, "Do you want to help me?"

Her mother nodded, sullenly, "Then wash your hands very well and bring me a chair in here."

Sarah covered the chair with a clean blanket and she and Mabel (the girl's mother) helped Elizabeth from the bed and sat her in the chair, a slow business with the constant contractions, but the breathing exercises seemed to help her some."

After settling Elizabeth, Sarah stripped the old sheets off the bed. As she did so, a couple of knives clattered to the floor. "What in the world?" she questioned.

Mabel answered, "Well, we had to cut her pain, you know."

Sarah nodded, it didn't hurt anything to have the knives there, if it brought Elizabeth comfort what did it matter? When she remade the bed, she slipped them back under the mattress. The grateful look on the faces of both didn't escape her. "Now, Elizabeth, we're going to have you get back in bed and I'm going to examine you. I'm going to try to time it between contractions, but it's going to hurt. I'm sorry. I need to see how this baby is laying."

After maneuvering her in the bed and getting Johnny and Mabel to hold her legs (the Granny had mysteriously disappeared) Sarah reached inside to check the baby. She found, as she expected, a breech baby. Instead of coming head first, this one turned bottom first. This life threatening situation coupled with the delay in calling her made it too late to call the hospital. Any more delay could cost the life of both mother and child. She knew she would have to turn the baby in some way. She showed Johnny and Mabel what to do on the outside of the stomach and did her part on the inside, eventually the baby turned even to fit through the birth canal.

"Elizabeth, I know you are exhausted, and in pain, but I need your help now. When I say 'push,' I want you to bear down, like you are using the bathroom and push hard while I count to five."

At Elizabeth's nod, she took her place at the foot of the bed, "OK, now push, one...two... three... four...five. Good job, Darling. It's going pretty past here. Rest for a second." After a minute she repeated, "Push, one...two...three...four...and five." After about twenty minutes, the baby slid into her waiting hands, other than being face up, he looked great. She cleaned his nose and mouth out then had Elizabeth push again and his shoulders and then body joined the rest of him. She wrapped him in one of the soft towels Johnny had given her and laid him on Elizabeth's chest. She let her have several seconds of looking at him, then said, "Now, Elizabeth, I have some good news. You are having another baby, you had twins in there all along!" At the stunned looks of the family she laughed, "Sometimes God gives us double blessings. Mabel, you take care of this little one, while we help the other one come."

They went through the pushing process again and Baby Emma soon joined Little John (as they named the first baby). Twins! Beautiful, healthy twins. Both Elizabeth and Johnny cried with relief and gratitude. Sarah delivered the after birth then took care of her patient. Because of the turning and the long labor, she feared the effects of a lot of blood loss and decided she would spend the night to make sure Elizabeth stayed stable.

That evening, Mabel fixed a large dinner of celebration. A vension roast with carrots and potatoes. It reminded Sarah of the meals she used to eat with Honey and her brothers and sisters. Afterwards, she took care of her patients, noted the bleeding was under control and fed Elizabeth a rich

327

warm venison broth with homemade bread chunks. Elizabeth and the babies were sound asleep in the bedroom and Johnny was asleep in a chair in front of the fireplace. Sarah took a cup of coffee and sat on the porch. The night had turned a bit cool, but the air was sweet and fresh, as only the deep mountains can be. Mabel sat down in the chair beside her, "Sarah, I'm sorry I didn't call you earlier. I was so afraid I was going to lose my daughter. After that minin accident where I lost my husband and two sons, I aint got nothing left. Thank you. Thank you for taking care of her and bringing my grandbabies into this world. I'm grateful to you. If there's anything I can ever do, please tell me and I will. We ain't got much money, but we'll pay your bill, I promise."

"Mabel, mostly people give me what they can. Some people bring me deer or firewood or carvings. I like it all." She knew people in these parts felt the need to pay, and wouldn't want to accept her charity, though she would have done her job for free.

"I got some quilts I made years ago, would you like a couple of those?"

"That would be perfect," Sarah replied, "I'm trying to make my home pretty and I love quilts, I just never get time to make them."

Mabel got up and went into the house, after a while, she emerged with three quilts, a gorgeous red and blue wedding ring, a crazy quilt, and a bowtie. Sarah was staggered at the beauty of the offerings, "Oh Mabel, they're wonderful! I love them, I can't take all three!"

"Yes, you can. It's one for each of the lives you saved today."

Sarah took the quilts and carefully rolled them to fit in her saddle bags. "Thank you so much. I will treasure them. Someday, I will put them on the beds of my children, and they will love them as much as I do."

Mabel smiled at her and they spent the rest of the evening talking amicably. When the time came for Elizabeth to give birth to the next six children, Mabel sent for Sarah with the first labor pains. In fact, she encouraged many women at the top of the mountain to send for Sarah and helped open many doors for her in places previously closed. In fact, one of Mabel's youngest daughters became a midwife herself and trained with Sarah.

Lavani

I smiled when I finished that entry. I knew my momma treasured those blankets; they were the ones that lay on the beds of my brother, my sister and me. They were worn now, but still warm and still beautiful. Momma never put something she loved away unless it outlived its usefulness.

The next few entries of Momma's journal detailed the progress and recovery of Elizabeth's babies. My favorite part is when she told about walking into the bedroom and finding them with their arms wrapped around each other. She also drew a picture of them, I marked that page, so that I could remove it and frame it for display, it was simply too beautiful to leave tucked away.

She talked about her developing friendship with Mabel and Elizabeth and how the twins came to call her Aunt Sarah. Emma had babysat Jay, Jayce and me upon rare occasion; funny, the connections we make in life.

Sarah

She cried as she sat pen to paper. Today, she helped bury a much loved and much wanted baby girl. Sophia came into this earth on a Tuesday, pink and strong. Sarah held her and kissed the top of her head, prayed for her well-being., then wrapped her in a blanket woven of such a delicate pink it looked almost white. While her momma slept, she held that baby close, smelled her fresh smelling head, rocked her and sang to her. That baby seemed to enjoy the cuddling, she curled up on Sarah's shoulder and laid her head right between her shoulder and jawline. She loved it. She loved her. She admitted her envy of Maria and Tom and their beautiful girl, Sophia.

331

Sarah left that morning never dreaming she would be back in just a few weeks to comfort grieving parents and prepare that dear baby for burial. Maria had laid Sophia in her bassinet, and she never awoke. Why give a couple such a wonderful baby, just to take it away? Sarah couldn't understand. She tried to remember that God controlled everything in life, but it seemed so cruel to give those parents such a beautiful gift, only to jerk it away from them.

Is it worse to have a baby and lose her or is it worse to never have a child? This question haunted her. Sarah could feel her soul crying out, "Why?" Perhaps, she should quit praying for a baby, maybe they caused too much pain. But, oh god, she wanted that love. She wanted to feel a baby grow inside her, kick her and move as she had seen and felt others. She wanted to give birth, then hold that baby close. She wanted to offer her breast to a baby and feel it suckle and watch it grow. She wanted to give Callaway sons to work on the farm with him, she wanted daughters to teach to weave and cook, to clean and work in the kitchen gardens. She wanted to hand down her knowledge of herbs. She just

332

wanted a baby. Her tears fell on the page of the journal, tears for baby Sophia, now an angel; and the angels she hoped waited to be her babies.

Lavani

Why does God give a child, a wonderful amazing child, then watch him suffer and die? Christian, my boy, had been sick from the first day. We didn't know why he stayed so sick, until the doctors diagnosed him with cystic fibrosis at six weeks old; but his illness never affected how I loved him. If anything, I loved him even more, because I didn't take the milestones for granted. The first of everything seemed doubly precious to me because my fear that the next milestone might not happen lived in the back of my mind. The day he received his permit, I cried in the Circuit Clerk office. I cried with the joy of knowing he reached this step he desperately wanted.

Feeling that all too familiar depression loomed too close, I decided to call Kevin. I seldom talked to him on the phone, we usually texted or emailed, or just talked in person. But, I needed to hear his voice and his laughter.

"Hello? Lavani? Is everything ok?" he answered.

I didn't consider the fact that he might think something bad happened to Momma when I called. I immediately reassured him, "We're ok. I was just feeling a little blue and wanted to hear your voice."

"Here I am, hear away," he said with a chuckle.

"Heard any good jokes lately?"

"Sure, 'why did the leopard not take a bath?'"

"Why?"

"He didn't want to be spotless!"

Jokes like that cracked me up. I laughed and felt so much better. We talked a while longer before saying good-bye. We didn't talk about anything serious, the storm the weatherman predicted for tomorrow, the way the tomatoes came on so suddenly, things that friends talk about, until the end.

"Lavani," Kevin said so solemnly that I stopped to listen, "I really need to tell you something. I hope it's not too soon for you." I held my breath. He continued, "I love you. I have always loved you. I will always love you. If there are previous lives, we were soul mates in all of them. I know you are still married, but I needed you to know how I feel."

I must have been speechless too long, "Lavani, are you still there?"

"I'm here. I just... Kevin, you are my soul mate. Always and forever. I loved you from before I was born and I will love you until the day that I die. I don't know what I am going to do right now. But, I know I love you."

He sang softly into the phone, "I don't know much, but I know I love you..."

I smiled, "Good night, Kevin." I hung up and lay on my bed for a long time, smiling at the ceiling, and for the first time in a long time, not questioning or overthinking anything. I just enjoyed knowing that this incredible man still loved me. I enjoyed knowing my heart felt light, without doubts or fears, just loved.

Later that night, I turned back to Momma's journal where I found a magazine article tucked between the pages. Apparently, the editors of the *Kentucky Living* magazine had completed a series of articles about "characters in the mountains."

Weaving Midwife Serves Appalachia

Part III: Mountain Characters

Although midwifery has been touted as slowly going out of style due to the proximity of new hospitals and better roads, there is one woman who is making a difference. Sarah Beth Thompson has served as a midwife for four years. By her estimation, she has helped deliver sixty-two babies, four sets of twins, and a calf in a crisis. What sets her apart, however, is the gift she gives to each child (not the calf).

"I learned how to weave as a child," she said, "it is a connection to my mother who passed away when I was young. It is also a way to relax in my spare time." Sarah probably does not get much spare time, as in addition to her midwifery duties, she is also a wife and active member of the local church. Her days consist of tending to the vegetable and herb gardens, taking care of the new home she and her husband, Callaway, just completed, and the many animals on site. However, when a person calls for help, she jumps into her car if the house is accessible by road, or onto her horse, Sweety, if the call comes from the mountain. Today, during our interview, I asked if we could talk just while she went about the normal day. I arrived at her home at 8:00, only to discover she had already been up for several hours. She said she would awaken usually around 5:30 to have some quiet time with her coffee and her Bible. Then, she would fix her husband's and, if it was a busy time, the field hands' breakfast. Today she had cooked for four, but some days she would cook for as many as ten or twelve. After cleaning the

breakfast dishes and straightening the house, we went outside to her extensive gardens. I helped her weed and hoe the vegetables, then went into the herb garden to "clean it up" as she called it. She worked efficiently, yet I could see the love she had for the plants. "God gave us so many good things to heal the body and mind," she said, "I hope we never forget the abundant gifts He has given." We left the herb garden to go into the flower garden where she again weeded and "dead headed" the flowers. She cut both of our arms' full and we took them into the house where she set them in every room of the house. She used old Mason jars with chipped tops, white pitchers and tiny bud vases. "I like to fill the house with flowers. They are so bright and cheerful and smell so good."

We went into her tidy kitchen where she sat a pot of soup beans on the back burner and then sliced a ham into thin pieces. She put this on a plate and in the refrigerator. "I also try to have something hot ready for lunch, unless it's just too hot outside. Callaway and the workers will come in around one and eat and rest under the shade tree for an hour. Today, it's just soup and sandwiches."

After the chores were finished, she sat at her loom and we talked as she worked on a delicate baby blanket. This one was pink and white with little strands of yellow throughout. "It reminds me of a flower bed," she said, "some little girl will sleep with this and dream of the gardens of Heaven." She showed me other blankets she had woven and stored. They ranged from light blues, to midnight blues, to greens and yellows and pinks and purples. "I always go back each day after a baby is born for a week. That way I can check on Mom and baby. After that week, I get a pretty good sense of a baby's personality and I can bring him a blanket to suit him individually. It is a pleasure to me to think of a baby using that blanket and, perhaps, giving it to her child someday."

I asked her how much she charged for the blankets and her services and she laughed. "Well, it doesn't really work that way around here. Not many people can afford a doctor or hospital, or anything really, that's one of the reasons they call me. Usually I'm paid in different ways. A rick of wood in the fall, fresh pork or beef, a handmade bench. Once, a family who was really hard on luck and had nothing to offer simply showed up to work a harvest with my husband and refused pay. Most folks don't like taking charity from anyone; they do what they can."

As we were settling into our conversation, a young man banged on the door. She rushed to him, then ran to get her bag, "I've got to go, a lady is in early labor. Please let yourself out." I watched as she stopped to speak reassuringly to him, then ran to the barn and came out on a beautiful brown horse. She turned its head to the mountain and was gone before I could fully admire the picture they made.

It's a different world, in Appalachia, but it is beautiful. As I prepared to take my leave, tired and full of information, I looked at my watch in amazement, it wasn't even 12:00.

I loved reading that article about my Momma. Everything in it was so true. I remember the bench, made by the Lawsons and have vague recollections of stern faced men unloading and stacking ricks of wood. Momma showed them where she wanted their offerings and then thanked them. She always made a point of telling them how she would use each item and how much she appreciated it. I never knew that people paid her this way, I just thought the people loved her. I laughed to myself. It's funny the way a child just takes things for granted. Our home stayed beautiful because of my momma and Daddy's hard work. She arranged everything in ways that celebrated the beauty of the art and nature. Daddy brought her things of beauty her found on the farm, a unique flower or branch, a heart shaped rock or a piece of quartz. He found such glory in the land, and shared it with her. She discovered the perfect places to tuck and display his offerings, on the book shelves, on counters, and in baskets and vases.

Momma always had fresh cut flowers in every room, I started to emulate that at my house when we first married, but allowed myself to get so busy with my family's' needs, I let it go. I missed the flowers. I missed their cheerful color and bright faces that seemed to smile at me. I wanted to brighten up my life with the things I loved. It didn't have to be expensive, I just needed to pay attention to what lay around me. God gave us so much to enjoy in nature it was time to start appreciating it. I decided to go to the store later in the day to get some flowers and put them in Momma's bedroom and bathroom, she would love that.

These days were hard. The middle of summer heat seemed more intense than usual, while Momma went downhill fast. She spent most of her time sleeping, either in her bed or in her recliner. Her visions of colors took place on a daily basis, I tried to write down in my journals the things she talked about, but it happened so often, I didn't get it all down. We took a walk every day, but lately the walks became slower and shorter. Most of the time, she knew us and talked to us, but sometimes, she didn't know anything. She constantly asked for Callaway. We assured her he would be along later. We knew he would be, and soon, so we tried to appreciate every single second we had left. Jay and Jayce came every weekend, and sometimes throughout the week. Her friends and her remaining sisters, Martha and Rose and brother, John, visited at odd times throughout the week. The company could be hard to deal with at times, but Momma enjoyed it and it gave her a break from us.

The best thing that happened during that time of waiting was a call from my Emily. Chatty and breathless with delight in her internship in New York, I could hear her smile through the phone. But, I could tell it wasn't just her job that put the zing in her voice. "Out with it," I told her. "Is it a boy?"

"You always know, don't you? How do you do that?" she exclaimed, laughing.

"Because I'm Mom, it's my job. Tell me about him." And she did. She described the man she loved.

"What's funny, Mom, is that he's from KY too. A little place named Milton. He's here on an internship with accountants who work on Wall Street. You'd think he'd be stuffy, but he's funny. He loves to dance and talk to people. But, he's good just staying in and watching a movie too. He makes me laugh."

I smiled, Nothing felt so sweet as first love. "He sounds wonderful. I hope to meet him someday soon."

After reassuring me that I would, she had to get back to work, so we hung up and I realized how much better I felt.

CHAPTER TWENTY:

I searched the house and found Honey to tell her I was ready to head out to the grocery store and she gave me the list of items we needed. She handed me the money, and I put it back into the coffee can when she wasn't looking. Momma had visitors today, and Hospice would arrive soon, so Honey planned to nap while I was gone. I put the top down on my car and headed into town. The town had grown so much from when I lived there, but I went to the market we always used. I wheeled my cart through the aisles, thankful for the homegrown foods Kevin brought us on almost a daily basis. He remained such a help with Momma, he always stayed a while and talked to her. We'd sit on the porch afterwards and just chat. I picked up a loaf of bread, and headed toward the aisle where the bacon would be, we'd enjoy some BLT's for supper. I was so engrossed in my thoughts, that I didn't notice the cart in front of me until I bashed into it. "Oh, I'm so…."

I had bashed into the cart of Kevin. He smiled at me, "Hi."

"Hi," I breathed back. I felt like that girl again. My heart tripped up and little and a blush lit my face. "Umm, I am sorry, I didn't meant to run into you." I saw this man almost everyday, why did I still feel all nervous and jittery?

"It's ok. No harm done. I just thought you'd be a better driver by now."

We both laughed, once he let me drive his beloved Mustang. I ran over the curb, off the road and almost hit a mailbox before he made me pull over. A long scratch down the side of the passenger door marred his perfectly shiny finish. Silently, I slunk into the passenger seat, while he stood outside with his back to me for a long time. Then, he slid into the driver's seat and turned up the music and sped out of there. Later, we laughed about it, after I helped him buff it out; but, he never did let me drive it again. "Yeah, I think it must just be you."

"Y'all ok today? If you need anything, just let me know. You know I'm glad to help out."

"Actually, I was thinking last night, why don't you bring your guitar and play for her. She'd really like that." I suggested

"I thought about it, but I didn't know if she'd enjoy the music or if it would bother her. You all keep it pretty quiet for her. I didn't want to cause any issues for her.

"No, most of the time she still enjoys music, sometimes it gives her a headache. If it does, I promise to tell you to stop. I think we'd all like it if you played. I'm making BLT's for supper. It's too hot for anything heavy. Come eat with us, too."

"Now, you know I've never turned down the opportunity for a meal you and your family made."

I laughed, "Except maybe the pork chops I made you the first time I tried to cook dinner for you. I burned them black and charred and the potatoes were half cooked and the gravy was lumpy and so thick you ate it with a fork."

He smiled at the memory, "That's alright, that's how I liked it. You can just keep trying to make it perfect," He winked at me and we each went on our separate ways.

Thoughts of him occupied my mind the rest of the trip as I paid for a couple bouquets of flowers and headed to the car. Some people said that young people could not experience true love. I disagreed. I knew Momma and Daddy's love had started early and shone bright and beautiful, and I knew I had loved Kevin with all my heart and soul.

We had broken up under some heart wrenching conditions. After dating for three years, rumors started circulating that when he dropped me off at curfew, he'd go into town and play pool at the pool hall. There, he met an ummm lady (and I use the term loosely) who would give him alcohol to drink and cigarettes to smoke. Eventually, she took him to bed. They had a wild fling, while I was oblivious. When I finally learned the truth, I told my parents I was going to spend the night with my best friend, Patti, who lived in town. She and I snuck out of her house and into the pool hall just in time to witness him kissing the bleach blonde bitch and being led to the door at the end of the building.

My heart was broken. At the time, that was the worst pain I had ever felt. The next day, when I told him what I'd seen, at least he was man enough not to deny it. "I'm glad you know, I didn't like sneaking around and I didn't know how to tell you." I slapped him. It was the only time in my life I have ever struck someone, and I didn't plan it, it just happened. He just looked at me for a long time, then walked to his car and got in and squealed tires as he took off. My momma and daddy were sitting at the kitchen table when I walked in. I tried to hide the tears, but they knew. Momma stood up and just grabbed me in a big hug while I sobbed on her shoulder. Daddy sat at the table just watching us. When I cried out, she sat me down at the table and made me a cup of tea, her cure for everything and my daddy just reached over and covered my hand with his. "Want me to kick his ass?" he asked

I laughed, even through the tears. He'd never offered to hurt someone. "No, I'll be ok."

Momma laid her hand on my back, "You will be, even though sometimes you think you won't. We love you." I drank my tea and went to my bedroom, removed all of his pictures from my walls and put them in a box under my bed. Then I laid down and slept for hours. When I woke with a headache and cried again, Momma heard and slipped into the room. I felt her lie down beside me, "I hate when you hurt, it hurts me." We just laid there.

I had forgotten about that. The times I really needed Momma, she was there for me. When Christian was sick, she took care of Emily and still managed to take care of me. She and Daddy did everything they could to ease my pain, there wasn't that strange sense of tension when I was hurting.

I pulled up into my driveway and unloaded the flowers and groceries and carried them in. Later, after putting everything away, I laughed when I discovered I had forgotten the bacon.

CHAPTER TWENTY-ONE:

Momma's journals continued to be full of stories now about the babies she helped bring into the world and the blankets she gave each. They were also full of her love for Callaway, and her hopes of having a baby with him. Year slipped into year and she became more and more desperate about giving him a child.

Sarah

I hate that Callaway has to work so hard, we have a good life, but who will keep this farm up when we are gone? A man needs sons, he needs to teach them to play baseball and build a little half court basketball court in the yard. He needs to bury his head under a hood with him, and teach that boy all about how engines function. A man needs

354

daughters, he needs them to kiss tenderly and feel protective over. He needs to pick flowers and play tea party and dolls. Why can't I give them to Callaway? I bring babies into this world all the time! Why can't I bring one into this world from me and him?

I try not to cry every month when I realize, again, I'm not pregnant. What is wrong with me? Why can't I conceive? Why? Why? Why can't I have a baby? Callaway and I are going to be great parents. I wonder if we should start thinking about adopting. I'm getting so old.

Lavani

These were a few of the many entries along those lines. Then the entries just stopped, for three months, she hadn't written a word, until about six months before I was born. The very last journal entry, of all her journals was just one sentence. "Oh God help me, I'm pregnant. What am I going to do?"

Stunned and confused I read that line over and over. She was finally pregnant and wasn't happy? Why? I looked through the stacks of journals and only the ones after I was born were there. This journal was only half full and it had been put away, all of her others were filled from the first page to the last before she went to the next book.

I found one that started with funny stories about me as a baby and how Daddy was enthralled with me; I guessed that was the next one she started by the date. But, why did she quit writing in her journals for all that time? I dug deep into the trunk, and found all of our baby books and albums with our school pictures in them. But, there was no continuation of the journal I was reading.

Sighing I laid my head on the edge of the trunk, then I stood up and shut the trunk. I had dinner to make, Kevin had called that afternoon asking if it was OK to come around tonight. I laid out the pork chops when I invited him to come and eat. I walked in and Momma was awake in her recliner. "Momma, I read all the journals. Thank you so much for letting me do that. It's really made me understand who you are. It's funny, a child thinks she knows her parents, but I didn't know you until now. You've given me such a gift.

She smiled at me, "Thank you for being interested enough to read them, I wasn't sure you would be. I've not always been the nicest to you. I lay in bed sometimes and think of the things I've said to you. I don't like them."

"Momma, I wasn't an easy child."

"Yes, but I should have let you know I loved you no matter what. I'm not sure I ever did. I should have let you know I liked you too. I know I never did. I'm blessed, Lavani, to call you my daughter. You truly are my grace. You make me proud."

I felt tears well up into my eyes. Wow. I never knew how much I needed to hear those words from her. I knelt by her chair and put my head in her lap. "I love you."

"I love you." She stroked my hair as I wept into her lap. When I quieted, she said, "I know you and Steve are having troubles, but you came here to help me anyway. I want you to know, I've saved all these years and you and your brother and sister will get a nice inheritance."

"Oh Momma, don't..."

"No, it needs to be said. I'm not going to be here much longer. I dream of Callaway every night, and I want to go be with him, I just have a few things to take care of first. I'm ready to trade this old body in and be out of pain. But, I needed you to know the whole story first."

"Momma, I still don't know, there's a journal missing."

"No, Dear, I just quit writing. I couldn't write about what happened at the time. But, several years ago, I did write it down for you. And, I have a letter I never opened from your father to you for when you learned your story."

I was fascinated, this was the stuff books were written about. "Really? Can I have them now?"

Let's get through dinner and company first. I will give you both tonight. Then you and I can talk about it tomorrow, I know you will have lots of questions, and for the first time in my life, I'm ready to answer them.

Momma seemed stronger that day than she had been for weeks. Kevin always made her laugh, and she enjoyed my pork chops, fried potatoes and gravy. He just laughed when he filled his plate, and said, "Now, that's a for sure improvement!" Then, he raved all through dinner about how good it was.

After his third helping Honey teased him, "Now, Kevin, you can come back anytime, you don't have to eat it all tonight." He smiled at her and winked. My momma laughed. It was so good to hear her laughing and teasing. After we finished, she and he took their coffee out to the front porch and talked quietly while Honey and I did the dishes and cleaned up. Honey said she was going to her room to watch some television, and I took a cup of coffee to go sit on the porch too. Momma had laid her head back and was sleeping in the outside chair and Kevin gazed out at the night, uncharacteristically silent and still.

"Hey," I whispered, "how long has she been out?"

"Just a little while, she was talking then she was sleeping. It's kind of like talking to my daughters when they were young," he smiled. "Why don't you sit down here with me? It is going to be a great night."

A breeze blew the scent of the flowers up onto the porch and the stars started to shine in the sky. A full moon already hung in the sky, even though the daylight still hung on. It was my favorite time of the day, twilight. The sky still looked bright, but a little hazy with the coming night. "I will, just let me get her into bed. If she stays that way much longer, her neck will hurt in the morning. Will you wait for me?"

"Sure, do what you need to do. I figure we need to talk."

I gently woke Momma and helped her into bed. I kissed her goodnight, snuggled her next to her Callaway pillow and tucked her in. As I left the room, I saw the small journal and envelope with my name on it by the side of her bed, so I picked them up and carried them into my room.

I stepped back out onto the porch, Kevin was strumming his guitar on the swing, I sat in the chair close by and just listened to him play for a time. Eventually, he asked, "So, are we ok?"

"Yeah," I responded. You were right, I shouldn't have asked you to come up there out of spite. I'm glad you didn't hold my anger against me."

"I'm right 97.75% of the time," he laughed.

"It's just that Steve had really messed up the house and he fired the lady I had paid to clean it and then he said I …" I tripped over my words I tried so hard to force them out. To let Kevin know what happened.

"Wait, Lavani, I don't want to get involved in this."

I gaped at him. What? Didn't want to get involved? Seriously? "What do you mean?"

"Well, I wouldn't know the whole story and I'd rather not know. Let's not talk about it."

What do you want to talk about? I asked incredulously? "What's acceptable to you?"

Apparently he missed my sarcasm. "Do you want to talk about the past? About sex? About day to day activities?"

"Let's just keep it fun. It's always been what we do best."

Unbelievable. "Yeah, that's what we do."

The silence stretched between us. "Ummm well, I need to get to bed, I have a lot to do tomorrow and I'm really tired."

"Sure, text me later if you want, I'd love some new good pictures." He leaned forward as if to kiss me, but I avoided his lips and laid a chaste kiss on his cheek and walked in the door. "Wow, all men are alike," I thought. "That's definitely NOT what pseudo husband would have said."

As I walked back inside, I found myself shaking my head. Did I really just hear that? Are all men as shallow as Steve? Maybe I could consider this a lesson learned and just move on. I decided to begin paying more attention to Kevin and my conversations. Perhaps, I read more into that snippet of conversation that I should have. I deathly feared getting involved with another selfish asshole. I might be over exaggerating.

I carefully locked the door behind me. We had never locked the doors before, but a series of break-ins in the area made us a bit more careful. I slept with my pistol beside the bed, and I knew Honey did the same. We weren't made of soft stuff.

I changed my clothes, washed my face and got ready to go to bed. When I walked in, the journal and letter laid there on my bed where I left them. I almost chose not to read them. I had so much to think about and dwell on. But finally curiosity overcame me, I wanted to know this deep dark secret about my birth. I opened the journal and began to read. It took me straight into a story from her midwifery days.

CHAPTER TWENTY-TWO

Sarah

Meg Johnson gave birth to a fine young man child. Born with a full head of black curly hair and a great set of lungs, he started howling the minute he entered the world and kept it up until she offered him her breast. Then he firmly latched on and suckled. She smiled down at him, tears in her eyes. Sarah knew she and her husband tried for a long time to get pregnant, almost as long as Callaway and she. 'He's so pretty,' Meg said. Her husband came in and the looks on their faces of love and awe made her cry. Sarah finished packing up her baby scale (he had weighed a whopping nine pounds!) and the rest of her items in her saddle bag. She knew just which blanket he was going to get. It was a midnight blue with lots of bold colors in streaks, a new technique she tried out earlier in the year. She checked her patients once again, made sure all the bleeding flowed right. It had been almost too easy of a birth, textbook really. The baby slept now with ridiculously long lashes laying against those plump cheeks. He was so pretty it almost hurt. She dropped a kiss on top of his head and bid everyone good-bye, assuring them she would be back the next few days in a row to check on everyone. If they needed her, she could be there fast, just let her know.

Todd Johnson walked her out to the barn where her horse had been walked, fed watered and housed after her arrival. She thanked him for the care of her beloved Sweety and prepared to mount. "Wait, please, just a moment, Ma'am." He twisted his hat in his hands. "We don't have much as of yet. I've got good prospects of working in the mines, I just don't want to go down under the earth, it makes me feel like I'm buried. We ain't got anything to pay you with."

"Don't worry about it," she said as she had said hundreds of time before. "We're OK. Don't go down in the mines, please, it's such a hard life." She thought about the men she saw on a daily basis with coal dust tattooed on their skin and their harsh coughs and looks of defeat.

"I'm gonna pay you I really will." He insisted.

"How about this? When you get around to it, will you carve me some bookends? I have lots of books on shelves at home and they keep getting knocked down. I saw those you did for Mrs. Wills and I just loved them."

"That ain't nothing' that's just playing around,"

"But they were beautiful. Made of mahogany in the shape of fairies behind the grass, I just loved them."

"Well, if yore sure that's what you want I can do that. But, I can't promise what they will look like, the wood just speaks to me, you know…"

"Anything you do is good, really."

Lavani

I thought, oh my gosh, I've seen those book ends! They were carved by the now famous Todd Johnson. His work has been shown in several museums as examples of beautiful folk art, even the White House displayed a piece of his work. No wonder Momma treasured them. They were gorgeous, made of yellow poplar, hers had a horse in full gallop on one with a woman on top, the other one showed the same horse peacefully walking with the same woman beside it. Her saddle bags were full on both and the woman portrayed, somehow, a quiet confidence. Amazingly, my mother knew him and apparently had one of his very first works. I turned back to the journal, almost dreading the part I was about to read. The hair stood up on the back of my neck and I knew something terrible was about to happen.

I was tempted to close it here. Momma's writing subtly changed, the words looks pushed together and slanted more. I saw deep emotion in the bold lines, like she had pressed so hard into the journal she tried to engrave the story. Before, her handwriting flowed lightly and elegantly upon the page. This entry appeared messy and almost harsh. I could tell she wrote with great emotion.

Sarah

He helped her mount her horse, "Are you sure yore gonna be ok? It's getting' dark. You can spend the night here."

"I appreciate it, but I'm used to the mountain, I just want to get home to my man." She smiled and waved and started Sweety on the path back down the mountain. Her thoughts were filled with the images of the baby and the way the Johnsons had looked at him. That's all she wanted, she thought, just one baby would do. Last night she and Callaway had made sweet love. After they finished, she cried in his arms. She wouldn't tell him what was wrong, but he held her for a long time, whispering how much he loved her. She prayed and prayed that she would become pregnant that night.

Suddenly, her horse stopped, she looked up, startled and, at first thought it was Callaway who was holding the bridle. It wasn't. This man had Callaway's face, but was thinner, more wiry obviously strong as he held the horse down from rearing. His eyes were chips of blue ice and there was a long black beard covering his face. She shuddered, he just felt evil. "Hello, Colton," she said.

He smiled, revealing several blackened teeth and spit a stream of tobacco at the ground, "Hello High and Mighty Half Breed."

"Don't call me that," she snapped.

"Now, how can you talk to yore dear brother in law like that? I saw yore picture in that fancy magazine and I've come all this way just to see you. I think you orter be giving me one of yore sweet kisses seein' as I'm here."

371

"Go away, Colton. Go back to whatever hole you crawled out of you filthy piece of shit."

His face darkened in anger and for the first time Sarah felt fear. She was out on the path going down the mountain, no one knew where she was and Callaway didn't expect her. She tried to jerk the bridle out of his hand so she could take off, but he held tight. "Now, half-breed, you ain't gonna treat me like that. Yore gonna treat me like a woman outta treat a man." So saying, he jerked the bridle down hard causing Sweety to stumble forward, then grabbed Sarah and threw her to the ground. Her ankle caught in the stirrup and twisted hard.

She lay there for a second, winded and a little dazed where her head had hit a rock. She tried to get her head together and get up to run. Sweety had taken off, but she figured she could make it into the woods and lose him until she could get to safety. She tried to jump to her feet, but stumbled when her ankle buckled under her. He grabbed her by the shirt, turning her to face him and slapped her in the face. Stunned, she kept fighting, kicking him and screaming until he simply shoved her down and put his boot on her throat. "Oh yeah, I'm gonna love this." He removed his belt, slinging it down until it cut against her chest. "Move and I will kill you, Bitch, and then I'll go to your place and kill that worthless piece of shit I used to call a brother." She stilled under the threat. He knelt beside her and ripped her shirt, reached inside her bra and squeezed both breasts painfully. She moaned in pain, "Oh yeah, Slut, we're going to have us a good time." She couldn't help it and tried to roll over and crawl away, he let her get a few feet then flipped her over and yanked her pants down until they entangled in her boots. He grabbed her arms and forced them above her head with one hand while he pulled his own pants down with the other. He rolled on top of her and jammed himself inside of her. She felt her skin ripping and screamed with the intrusion and the pain. He continued to shove himself in her over and over again until she was whimpering instead of screaming. She had never known such pain and humiliation. When he had spent himself, he rolled off of her with a loud moan. She rolled away from him into a fetal position, trying to force herself off the ground, but hurting too much to get far. Finally, she sat and pulled up her pants then stood to find her ruined shirt and bra. He just watched her from the ground. "Where you goin' in such a hurry? I thought me and you could stay here awhile, wait on that man of yours. Going so soon?" Standing he grabbed her, throwing back his head when she flinched away. Here, give this to my brother, and bending his head he tried to kiss her. She spit in his face, then the pain and darkness exploded beside her ear when he punched her.

When she came to, Sweety grazed nearby, it was near the morning of the next day and she was alone. Groaning with the pain, she forced herself to mount her horse and head down the mountainside. She prayed the entire way that Callaway would not be home. Dragging herself in the front door, she cried with relief when she saw the note on the table saying he had to go to town and wouldn't be home until late that night. She pulled herself to the phone, called another midwife who would cover for her and then Honey. "Please come," was all she said.

"I'm on the way."

When Honey got there, she found her, almost unconscious in a steaming hot bath where she tried to scrub away Colton's touch. "Oh Darling, Oh Baby," Honey kept whispering to her as she helped her out of the tub, saw the scratches all the scrubbing had made on her skin, the dark bruises on her breasts and stomach and thighs, the black eye and busted lip and cut on the back of her head. Crying, Honey doctored the wounds, wrapped her ankle, helped her into a warm nightgown and slipped her into the bed. She went to the kitchen and fixed her a cup of tea. Bringing it to the room, she sat on the edge of the bed. "Who did this to you?"

"No one, I fell from my horse."

"Who did this to you? I know when a woman's been hurt that way."

"Honey, you can't tell Callaway, he will kill him." In desperation, Sarah grabbed her arms, "please please help me convince Callaway I fell from my horse. He'll kill him, he'll go to jail. He'd never be able to live with himself."

375

She begged until Honey reluctantly agreed, "I'll do what I can, but you're wrong not to tell him, he deserves to know. It was Colton wasn't it?"

Sarah nodded in fear and shame.

That night, when Callaway came home and heard about her "accident" he rushed into the bedroom. She assured him she felt fine, just sore, and fell almost immediately back asleep. When he crept into the bed that night, he stayed careful to avoid touching her. She had nightmares that night, and replayed everything over and over in her sleep, when she awoke, she was sobbing and he was holding her gingerly, "Sarah, please let me take you to the hospital. You're hurt worse than you think."

"Callaway, I'm a nurse, I know what to do. It's fine." She lay still until his even breathing told her he slept. Quietly she limped out of bed and into the bathroom, she wanted to get her shower finished and dressed before he could see her bruises. Stepping into the hot shower was a torture almost, the water was harsh against her abraded skin and scratches. As she stood under the spray, trying to find a place that eased the pain, the shower curtain opened.

Callaway stood there, looking at her. His eyes swept down her body and back up, noting each bruise, each scratch and cut on her body. Silently, he showed her the towel he held. She stepped up and he very gently dried her, then went to the bathroom and got her loosest warmest gown. Still silently, he walked behind her to the kitchen and set the coffee pot onto the stove. "That's one hell of a horse throw, Sarah." He broke the silence. "Now, why don't you tell me what really happened."

"Sweety saw a snake, and she reared up…"

"You never did lie worth a fuck, and you talk in your sleep. Tell me what happened."

She broke down and told him the truth. How a man had hurt her and raped her. She never mentioned his name though.

Callaway's face was white and tight with worry and anger. "You say you don't know who did this to you?" His voice was dangerously quiet, his eyes were hard and sparked with anger and concern.

377

"No, I didn't know who he was, he was just some stranger...."

"Then why did you cry out 'Colton, No!' in your sleep?"

She could only stare at him in anguish. He dropped his head into his hands. "My brother did this? My brother hurt you like this?"

She nodded, fearful of his actions. "I didn't want to tell you, I don't want you to go after him and maybe get killed or hurt. I need you too much."

"It's my job to protect you. If I can't protect you, I need to take care of who hurt you. That's what a husband does."

"It's your job to stay with me, to protect me by taking care of yourself. Please, please don't go after him, I can't stand to think of you around that gang of his." She broke down, sobbing and incoherently begging him to not avenge her.

He took her in his strong arms, lightly rubbed her back and soothed her as best as he could. When she wore down, he carried her to the bedroom where he lightly put her to bed. For the next few weeks, he tended to her as gently as a nursemaid, Honey went home, glad to know he knew, and Sarah came to trust the feel of a man's hands again. Late in the night a few weeks later, she turned to him and they made love.

She discovered, three months after the attack, that she was pregnant. She would never know for sure which man was the father. She never knew who helped her create this wonderful baby. It haunted her when she looked into her Lavani's eyes; who would she grow up to be most like? Would she be loving and kind like Callaway? Would she be cruel and heartless like Colton? Would she be more like Sarah and seek to serve others? Only time could tell.

Lavani

Oh my God. Tears streamed down my face as I finished reading the journal entry. She has gone forty-five years looking at me and not knowing who my father is. I'm either a product of rape and hate, or a product of great love. And, I look like my dad. I have the black hair and the face shape of the Thompsons, no wonder, no wonder…. I cried until I couldn't cry anymore.

My personality didn't match any of the three. I grew up more introverted, interested in books and schoolwork, a bit of a tomboy. I played softball in my spare time, in fact, we used to laugh that I was a boy until I turned fifteen and discovered Kevin. Even he and I did mostly guy stuff. We passed ball in the yard frequently, we rode his little dirt bike around the farm, we went to baseball and basketball games on dates. I didn't become more girly until after I gave birth to Emily. I swear, she came out with sparkles and a hot pink dress.

I understood, now, why Momma watched me so closely. I thought about one time when I ran into the catcher in my rush for home plate. The girl fell and hit her head hard on the ground. I didn't know why Momma said she was proud of me when I stopped and helped her up (after tagging the bag of course) and checked on her. Now, I knew she anxiously looked to see if I enjoyed causing that pain. I sure didn't.

I wanted to go to her and hug and love her, but I didn't. She would be tired and upset, confused if I came in. The two blankets that were mine made sense now; Momma couldn't decide which to give me, because she didn't know who my father was. There was tension always between us because she didn't know if she hated me or loved me.

I decided to keep both blankets. Although I was sure that Colton was not my dad, I knew that his act of cruelty affected my entire life. I would keep the blanket to remind me, that even though she certainly knew how to do it, my mother did not force an abortion to lose me. She made a conscious decision to live with the doubt and the pain of looking me in the face every day of her life, because she loved me. She kept me, no matter what. I was

381

the result, the reminder, of her rape, yet she loved me and cared for me. All my life I had been pro-life, but I struggled with the question of rape. I still did, but I felt grateful that my mother didn't.

I knew I wouldn't sleep that night, so I went to the kitchen and started the coffee pot. 3 a.m is a lonely time. I drank coffee and stared out at the darkness, watching the heat lightning flash on and off. I had carried my Daddy's letter in with me, but I hesitated before opening it, I didn't want to find out anything more on this night. Finally, though, I did and I found a letter addressed to me.

Dearest Lavani,

If you are reading this, your mother has decided to tell you the truth. I hope she does, because I think the truth sets you free. I wanted you to know, first and foremost, you are MY daughter. Not just because I want it so, but because it is so. You are blood of my blood, flesh of my flesh and I love you with all of my being. I am proud of who you are and what you have become. I hope after reading this you are still proud of me and you understand what I did and why I did it. It's a man's responsibility to take care of his women, and I did what I had to do.

I was patient after I found out about the attack on your mother. I knew Colton would have rushed right into a situation immediately, so I wanted to take the advantage of preparation away from him. When you were about eight weeks old, I had to go to my mom's house. She and my step dad were feeling bad and I wanted to go and do some repairs around her place. I left Sarah and you at home with lots of kisses and Honey to take care of you. I promised to be back when all the jobs were done, and I took off.

I did go to my mom's and I did repair the roof and the chicken coop and a few other odds and ends. When everything was done, I took my stepfather out in the yard and told him what happened and what I intended to do. He wanted to go with me, but I wanted someone to know where I was, so that if I was killed, they would know where to find my body. I didn't want to tell my mother, she'd try to talk me out of it, and I had to protect you both. I didn't want to involve any of my friends, I didn't trust them not to tell someone. But, I knew Joe. I knew I could trust him, and I knew he'd do the same thing to protect my mother.

He never did tell a single soul. I walked up into the mountain early the next morning. I knew where I would find Colton and his gang. In my pocket was my pistol and on my hip was my hunting knife I used when I dressed game. I was prepared to use one or both. I walked into their camp without any kind of alarm raised. They were all there. Lying around on the ground, hung over and nasty dirty. Some of them had their whores with them, I woke the women and told them to leave. You should have seen the rats scatter from that ship. By that time, the entire camp was awake and Colton was leaning against a tree watching me.

I started walking towards him and he smiled at me, I punched him square in the face, he fell like a tree. I straddled him and yanked his shirt up, *"Come on you fucking coward. Why don't you fight me? Or can you only handle tiny women who can't fight back. I stood up, pulling him to his feet and punched him in the stomach and then in the face again. Every time he fell, I pulled him up again, I could only see hot red behind my eyes. But, one of his men finally stepped between us.*

"Callaway, you proved your point. If you ain't gonna kill him, you better go." I looked at Colton, being held up there by two of his men, his face was covered in bruises and blood and cuts. My hands were raw, and the few places he had hit me felt a little sore. I didn't even realize until then that he had gotten some punches in.

I walked right up to him and got in his face, hatred glared back out of the one eye that wasn't swollen shut. "If you ever show your face around my place, my family or my wife again, I will kill you on sight. I will not ask questions, I will not give you a chance for an explanation and I will not stop this time until you are dead."

He spit in my face. Jesus, the man was beaten half to death and barely hanging on and spat in my face. I wiped it off, wiped it on his shirt and turned to leave. I had gone about three steps when the hair stood up on the back of my neck, I heard a rushing noise and turned around to see him charging me with a knife. He jumped on me, that's the scar on my arm, and we fell to the ground. When I got up, the knife was sticking in his chest and he was gasping his last breath. Lavani, I left. I didn't stay to see him finished, I left. I went to my mom's home, showered off and she fixed up my arm. Hours later, the sheriff came by to tell her that Colton was dead and the men swore he had been killed by some stranger. I killed my own brother.

I tell you this for two reasons. I want you to know that I protected your momma with all I had, I would have died for her on that mountain. I might be an evil man for what I done, but it's done. She and you are both safe. You never have to fear him anymore.

I never told Sarah. I hope she never knows. It's your choice, of course if you will tell her, but I'm asking you not to. She has suffered, she has nightmares and flinches if I touch her unexpectedly. I could kill him all over again when that happens. But, we are working through it, with love and with hope. You, our "grace," brought us incredible joy. You are mine. You are hers. You are a product of us.

I love you.

Dad

CHAPTER TWENTY-THREE:

Lavani

I folded the letter and put it back in its envelope, then placed it in the small journal. I put them both into the trunk, at the bottom underneath all the other journals. I was stunned. I didn't even have the ability to think at that moment, only act. I went back to the kitchen. When Honey came in, I was standing at the window staring at the rain falling outside in steady streams. "I guess she told you?" were the words she greeted me with. At my nod, she walked over and rubbed my back, "It's hard to know, but you needed to." Again, I nodded. She sat at the table with her coffee and we stayed in silence, thinking our own thoughts for a long time.

"Honey, have I thanked you for helping Momma? I don't mean now, but all through her life. You've always been her caretaker and her friend."

Her words were simple, "Well, she's mine."

I understood what she meant by that. I cared for Christian through every breath he took, from the first one when they laid him on my chest, until the last one with my hand on his chest. It didn't matter that it was hard, he was mine. He is mine. Always and forever, he is mine. My eyes filled with tears as I felt something release a little bit inside me. He was a precious gift, a shooting star, always I would love him and miss him; there would never be a time I wouldn't. Rachel still mourned inside me, she always will, but I finally understood, he will always be mine.

I pushed back from the table, "Momma sure is sleeping late today. I'm going to go see if she needs something. We have so much to talk about today, I hope it's a good day." I walked into her room and gently bent over to awaken her, "Momma. Momma?"

She lay in the bed with a small smile on her face. Her skin felt cold and a little stiff when I touched her. I screamed, even though we expected this to happen. Honey came running in and, together, we called 911. We never would have that talk. Once she was assured I knew the truth, she decided to go home with Daddy.

As they always say, the rest of that time was a blur. Through the ambulance and coroner, contacting Jay and Jayce, to the funeral home I simply placed one foot in front of the other and did what had to be done. Momma made it as easy as possible for us. In her top drawer was a list of the items she wished to wear and she had already set up her service with the local funeral home. The people of our little town brought food and stories, and some brought the blankets she had made just for them. It was a time of celebration of an extraordinary life rather than a time of sadness. She had lived well and made many friends. Isn't that what we all want to be able to say at the end of our lives? We lived well and loved much.

After the funeral, a large crowd came back to the house to eat and talk, an old country tradition I was thankful to follow. Escaping the confusion for a bit, I went into my bedroom and took off my shoes and just laid back on the bed. I hate funerals. I hate death. The night before, when everyone left the funeral home, I stayed for a little while with Momma. I knew only her body lay there, but I hoped her spirit could hear me.

"Momma," I said, "Momma, I love you. I am so thankful we've had the last bit of time to understand each other. I can't believe what you went through. I'm not sure I could have loved me at all. You did a good job. I'm sorry you were hurt; but, I firmly believe that Daddy is my true father, my blood father. I hope you found that out as soon as you crossed over. I know he waited for you and you are together. Please, Momma, please give Christian a hug for me. Tell him how much I miss him every single day. Tell him I love him and how proud and blessed I was to be his mother on this earth. I wait for the day I can see him again, and you and Daddy. Be at peace. I love you. I love you." I wished I could have talked to Christian like this, back then; but my words stuck behind a huge lump in my throat at that time. All I could get out was, "Thank you, we are fine, we'll be ok." In many ways, this brought that back home to me. Yet, there remained a sense of peace here, a sense of a life well-lived and a death desired. None of those feelings

After I lay there a little while, Steve knocked softly on the door frame then came in. He looked handsome in his black suit and tie. I might be angry with him, but I knew he grieved as well. He sat on the edge of the bed and I let him take my hand. He always did well in times of crisis or sorrow.

"Vani, I'm sorry about your Momma, she was a good lady and I loved her," I knew he did. In some ways she had educated him far beyond his own mother. She never forgot his birthday, and listened to him when he needed someone. He teared up and his voice became thick with his sorrow, "This world lost an amazing woman."

I nodded. He didn't even know how strong she was, no one but I would ever know that. I thought about telling him what I learned, but decided to keep it to myself. The silence between us felt companionable this time, not tense, until he broke it, "Vani, are you coming home?"

The question struck me. I still didn't know what I was going to do. Going home with Steve was the safe choice, the one guaranteed not to rock the boat or cause anyone any problems. I answered honestly, "Steve, it depends."

"On what?"

"On where I fall on your priority list."

"What do you mean?"

"It means, are you willing to change anything you do?"

"What are you talking about?" His voice was a little irritated.

"I mean this. I have not been a priority in your life in a very long time, maybe never. You've always put your own needs and wants ahead of mine. I can fight with another woman, I can help you rehab from drugs or alcohol, I can do almost anything to keep you, but I cannot compete with yourself."

"I don't understand what you are saying."

"OK, I will put it simply. Are you willing to limit your ball playing, spend weekends with me, go on vacation with me instead of golf trips, turn off the baseball game to talk to me? Are you willing to possibly see a marriage counselor to see what we can do to reconnect? Are you willing to make me a top priority in your life?"

He thought for a long time, "No."

"Then you have your answer."

He stood up and left the room, quietly. I couldn't even find the tears to mourn my marriage at this time. I waited for the sense of devastation and remorse to fill me, many of my friends who divorced said they felt these immediately afterwards. I waited for the anger to bubble up and choke me. Nothing. I realized I just felt sad. And relieved.

I joined the rest of the mourners in the kitchen, noticing that Steve left after our talk. That was ok. Later, Kevin showed up and we chatted some. I didn't know what to do about him. I decided to wait until much later to think about it. I had lots of time.

PART THREE:
EPILOGUE

Soon after the funeral, I contacted a realtor who found me a small condo. I looked at it and loved it. A small two bedroom place on the ground floor, it was in a facility with a swimming pool and a fitness center. There was a room and bathroom for Emily when she came home and a large master suite for me. The kitchen was small, but I'd only be cooking for me now, mostly, so that was ok. It came furnished, so I didn't have to shop for anything other than personals at that point and that suited me just fine.

In the following months, Jay, Jayce and I went through our parent's home and picked out what we wanted and what we intended to sell. I ended up with, among other things, the beautiful book ends and the quilt from my bed. I knew I would treasure them because of the stories I read, not just because of their beauty. No one wanted the farm, so Kevin offered us a fair price and we took it. He was going to farm the land and rent the house out. He offered to let me live there for free, if I wanted. I knew he was offering more, but I didn't accept. Living with Steve made me hesitant about taking things on face value. I still found myself questioning whether or not I would ever make Kevin's priority list. However, before I settled into any kind of commitment, I needed to know myself. I loved him, I always will, but I knew I needed to learn to love myself.

Honey decided to move into an assisted living home near me. I visited her every day, but she went downhill very fast. The fragility I had noticed earlier in the summer became more and more pronounced. Not long after Momma passed away, the nurses found Honey. She suffered a heart attack in her sleep and peacefully left this world. I think she died of a broken heart.

Momma left each of us a sizable nest egg and after the sale of the farm and equipment we were pretty well set. It was a blessing to me, I'm taking early retirement next year. I'm going to travel on my own for a little bit, I might take some culinary courses. I'm starting to dream again.

Steve, as I anticipated, has been a total ass about the whole divorce settlement. Luckily for me, he went into the courtroom with an attitude and told the judge that I had never really worked, all I had ever done was teach and take care of the kids, since he worked he owned all of the marital property and nothing should be given to me. He also made a stupid remark about women stealing from men through the years. So, I ended up with a very nice alimony check, half of the sale of the house and half of his 401k. He makes a point of mailing the alimony check exactly one week late, so it arrives the day before he would get in trouble. I don't care. I wouldn't have even asked for alimony if he hadn't been such a jerk. My lawyer had said to put it in the paperwork as a point of negotiation, so we did. It comes in handy, though. I've put that money in a bank account to pay for Emily's wedding.

That's the other wonderful thing. My Emily is totally and completely in love with her Landon. Every time she speaks of him, her blue eyes sparkle, it reminds me of my momma's sparkle for her Callaway. They are going to get married next summer after they graduate. She has already designed her own wedding gown and started sewing it. I promised to help sew on beads and pearls, but she just laughed at me, "Remember, Mom, the pastor calls you the 'anti-craft' for a reason."

She has promised me a beautiful dress to wear, something in blue she said. I can't wait. I can't wait because I can see the love she wears for him, like a woman wears a beautiful shirt. She loves him with a single minded focus that reminds me of my love for Kevin in an earlier time. I hope and pray she always feels this love.

She asked both Steve and me to walk her down the aisle. We both willingly put aside our differences for that. We know what it is to lose a child, to not know this experience, and neither of us would ruin it for her. Steve might not be the best husband in the world, but he loves her. We love her enough to never make her choose between us.

After living with Momma that summer, I lost a little bit of weight; I kept it up. I think much of my weight problem revolved around living with Steve, I eat when I am stressed or unhappy. Now, I follow a diet plan and work out at the apartment complex fitness center four days a week. I walk to my job in good weather and have started taking some pride in my appearance. One of my friends hooked me up with her beautician, and after spending a whopping $125 I walked out of there with the grey gone, my eyebrows shaped, a new cut and make up on. I was asked out three times that day in the mall!

I see and talk to Kevin frequently. We have become lovers again. He'd like to go farther, but I won't. I need to know that I'm choosing this because I want it, not because I am scared to be alone. Besides, it's nice to have a lover on the sly. He shows moments of stupid selfishness, but then, so do I. I love him in a different way now. Gone is the bright eyed hope of Prince Charming, but I like this love better. It feels richer and warmer, we are learning to love past the flaws and mistakes and into the core of each other.

God and I? Well, we're talking. Turns out, He never left me, just sat quietly by while I shut Him out. I'm still pretty mad though, so I don't know if our relationship will be better, but I'm trying to be quiet and listen a little more than scream and yell. After all, three of my most beloved are with Him now, I'd like to see them again one day.

So that's it. Just a normal life. This is my happily ever after and I like it. I like being me, being on my own and independent. I enjoy being me, for the first time in my entire life.

But, the important thing is, I now know for sure, my mother loved me.

Made in the USA
Lexington, KY
09 March 2014